Mrs Durham's

© Ann Perry

For my Mum with love.

My thanks must go to Dave Hayes, he has worked so hard to get this book published for me. He has also designed the wonderful book cover.

My muse, Phil McEleney, some of these stories would never have happened without his suggested topics, and, specifically, Gang Killer. His knowledge about American cars was an enormous help. Thanks Phil.

Foreword

When I was asked to write the foreword for Ann Perry's new book I was pleased, and indeed honoured to accept. She writes with a honesty and warmth that is rare in this day and age. Ann is very much a 'people watcher'. She gets inside the characters mind and lays it out before us like a welcoming picnic blanket on a summers day. She writes with humour and pathos in equal measures, but never gratuitously so. I keep coming back to that word - honesty. It sums up her writing so well.

At the time I was writing my own first book, Ann was in the same Facebook group. She was always one of the people whose feedback I valued the most. If ever anyone deserved to break through and become popular, it is Ann.

Each and every one of these stories is a little gem in itself, and I have thoroughly enjoyed reading them. I hope you do too.

The Street Entertainer

I sit and watch him most days. He turns up and sets out his stall every day at eight thirty a.m. I say stall, it's not a stall, that's just a figure of speech. I think he's homeless, he throws a blanket on the ground and sits on it, sharing with a sweet, little, black and white dog of indeterminate breed. He plays with the little dog for a while, then 'starts work.' He's a busker and produces the most beautiful sound. He has an extensive repertoire. He isn't aware that I watch him. He cannot see me, although I am only a matter of yards away. He plays his saxophone perfectly, and the sound he produces is magical, you think it can't get any better. Then he removes his saxophone, and he sings. That is when the real magic begins.

His clothes are grubby, and his shoes are missing their laces. He is bearded, making it difficult for me to put an age to him. His hair is long and somewhat unkempt, but it is a vibrant, corn colour, and very shiny. I am amazed at how he can have such clean looking hair when the rest of him, quite frankly, isn't. As I watch and listen, I wonder how he fell on such hard times. He has obviously been very well trained. No one could be this good without classical training, at least, I wouldn't have thought so.

At what stage did everything go wrong for him? The street is starting to get busy, commuters hurry past him, barely glimpsing in his direction, never mind standing and listening. Shoppers amble by, staring in shop windows. Unlike most buskers, this man has no backing music. When he plays his saxophone, it is the only sound you hear. The same with his singing, his voice is pure, and pitch perfect.

What I admire most about the street musicians talent, is how adept he is at changing his style of music. His sheer versatility. I am listening to him sing Leonard Cohen's Hallelujah, and I notice a little girl watching him intently. She is holding her mother's hand. Mum is busy chatting to someone and quite oblivious to the sound of this remarkable voice. The busker sees the little girl looking across at him, he stops mid-song and winks at her. The wheels on the bus go round and round, round and round, round and round, the wheels on the bus go round and round, all day long. The little girls face suddenly lights up, and a massive grin spreads across her pretty face. She knows that one.

The morning moves along, and the street is busy. I notice a few people show their appreciation, and generosity, towards the man entertaining them, and rightly so. He deserves the recognition of his audience. Someone walks over and pops a few treats down for the little dog. He immediately wolfs them down, then moves over to the bowl of water that a thoughtful shopkeeper provides every day. A police officer wanders past, he stops for a while and listens. The musician's voice sings out Nella Fantasia. The uniformed man seems to be lost in his own world, a beautiful world for those few moments he listens. But duty calls, and he turns to walk away, takes a few steps, puts his hand in his pocket and pulls out some loose change. He walks back and drops it in the plastic container. He bends down and fusses the dog, and reluctantly it seems, walks away.

An American couple, tourists I presume, stop to take a photo of the street entertainer in full flow. 'Hey Bud,' d'ya know Baker Street?' The tourist shouted the question at the music man. I am guessing he means the music and not the address of Sherlock Holmes. The saxophone sounded perfect as the busker played his first request of the day. The tourist seemed well impressed and took his wallet out and rewarded the man generously.. at least a fiver, but maybe even ten.

It's lunchtime, someone usually brings the busker a sandwich, a pie, or sometimes a burger. He always has a bottle of water at hand. A swig here, a swig there. Sensible, he needs to keep those vocal chords lubricated. Ah, here we go. A lady has just come out of Greggs and is looking in his direction. I think a nice steak bake could be on the menu for him today.

Early afternoon always sees the street quieten down a little, but still, he entertains us. The little dog is lying down now, afternoon nap time for him. Easy listening seems to be required most afternoons, today is no different. No one seems to be in a rush, they have a little time to spare. 'Somewhere' from West Side Story. 'Where is Love' from Oliver, and 'Bring Him Home' from Les Miserables, all sung in the beautiful, clear voice of the street entertainer. By mid-afternoon, the children are coming from school. The busker does not forget them either. The kids gather around him, and they play with the little dog as they listen to the songs that maybe he heard to as a boy. 'The Owl and The Pussycat', 'Little Boy Fishing off a Wooden Pier', and 'I Know an Old Lady Who Swallowed A Fly'.

As the afternoon draws to a close and commuters are heading back home, he plays a couple more tunes on the saxophone. His 'Summertime' easily matches that of the great Charlie Parker, then he somehow drifts into the gentle tones of Misty, so beautifully played long ago by Stan Getz. This man could play with the best.

Well, I'm heading off now. I had better tell you who I am before I go. I'm a newspaper seller. That's my hut there. You see, I can see the street entertainer from my little seat, but he would have to be facing a different way to see me. Going home now, I hope the busker and his dog find a bed for the night. We will be back tomorrow, to do it all again... God willing.

The Airman

The young airman in his RAF uniform was so handsome, and Lizzie could see him clearly in her mind's eye. She lay in her hospital bed. She knew she was dying, and that her time left on this earth was short. She smiled to herself, she'd had a good innings and a good life. She had been happy and had lived the life she chose to live.

Her mind wandered back to 1943. It was wartime, but life had been fun. Every day was lived as though it may be the last, which of course, it could have been. She remembered the first time she saw Bill Jenkins; it was in the local dance hall, and, like her, he was there with a friend. Friday and Saturday were the highlights of the week. Dance nights. Good music, good friends, budding romances and a chance for everyone to forget the war for a while and have a good time.

Flo, Lizzie's best friend, nudged Lizzie and directed her head in the direction of two uniformed young men who were stood a little bit further into the dance hall. 'He's a bit of alright Liz' Flo said, 'and he's with a pal.' Lizzie glanced across to where Flo had been looking, and there he was. Easily six foot tall, and dark-haired, Bill Jenkins looked directly at Lizzie and smiled. A broad grin, and sparkling, crystal blue eyes. Lizzie was smitten. All this packaged in an RAF uniform.

'Oh Flo,' stammered Lizzie, 'he's gorgeous, and I think he and his friend are coming over.' 'Hello girls, I'm Jim, this is Bill, he's the ugly one.' Jim laughed as he said it. He was a very confident young man. 'Hello, I'm Flo, this is my best friend, Lizzie.' Flo hadn't taken her eyes off Bill as she had introduced herself and Lizzie. Bill hadn't taken his eyes off Lizzie. 'What you drinking girls?' Enquired Jim. Bill still hadn't spoken. 'Cat got your tongue Bill?' Jim shoved him. 'No, I was just about to ask Lizzie if she'd like to dance with me.' Bill answered with the beautiful lilting accent of the Welshman that he was. Lizzie felt her face go pink. 'Oh yes, I'd love to,' said Lizzie, suddenly finding her voice too.

If Flo was upset at being passed over in favour of her friend she didn't show it. She linked her arm with Jims and suggested they also had a dance. At the end of the evening, it was clear that Lizzie and Bill had eyes for no one but each other, but it was time to go. Lizzie back to her home in Folkestone where she still lived with her parents and Bill had just over two miles to walk to RAF Hawkinge where he was stationed. It was from there he flew his Spitfire. He had only been there a few days, arriving on Saturday 21st August with 91 Squadron. Their posting was until Saturday 18th September. The squadron would then be posted elsewhere. Where of course was never divulged until much nearer the leaving date.

Outside the dance hall, Bill took both of Lizzie's hands in his own and asked if he could see her again, he thought he could get a pass for tomorrow night, Saturday. 'I'd love to Bill,' Lizzie wondered if she sounded a bit too keen. She needn't have worried, Bill seemed pleased when he responded. 'That's good, shall we go to the pictures?' They arranged to meet at 6 30pm outside the Folkestone local picture house. 'May I kiss you goodnight Lizzie?' Lizzie nodded her head, and Bill gave her a gentle peck on her cheek. They said goodnight and went their separate ways, each with their friend who had discreetly stood a little way from them while they arranged their next date.

Lizzie was running desperately late, she had finished her shift way after she should have because another wretched air raid warning had sounded, and everyone had to run to the nearest air raid shelter. Lizzie worked as a clippie on the East Kent Bus Company buses. She loved her job. Chatting with the passengers, helping young mums with children on and off her bus and of course, helping the elderly with their shopping bags, though with rationing they were not as heavy as they used to be. Still, she was home now and had to get ready for her hot date.

She had chosen her dress, a pretty floral print, fitted, to show off her trim figure. Lizzie brushed her shoulder-length, wavy, auburn hair till it shone and added a dab of lipstick to her lips. She pinched her cheeks to give them a touch of colour and slipped into her dress. Almost ready to go, just her shoes to pop on, brown court shoes with a comfortable heel. As she opened the front door, she grabbed her gas mask off the hall stand and shouted to her parents that she was going now and would see them later.

It was only a ten-minute walk to the town centre, and Lizzie would just about make it on time. Bill had arrived in the town early, he didn't want to be late for his first date with Lizzie. He stood outside the picture house and rechecked his watch. Six twenty-eight. He had been there for the last twenty minutes, good job it was a lovely evening, he thought to himself. Lizzie turned the corner into the street where the picture house stood and immediately saw Bill standing there, waiting for her. Her heart skipped a beat. She had forgotten just how handsome he was. Bill looked up and spotted Lizzie walking towards him, he raised his arm and waved to her. She waved back, and as she got closer to him, in unison they said 'hello'. Each smiled, and Bill said 'I have checked to see what film is showing, it should be good. Katharine Hepburn and Spencer Tracy in Woman of the Year.'

'Perfect,' said Lizzie. 'I love Spencer Tracy.'

'Oh,' said Bill, laughing, 'competition already is it?'

At that precise moment, the air raid siren went off. Without thinking Lizzie grabbed Bill's hand and shouted 'come on Bill, I know where the shelter is.' They emerged forty minutes later not knowing what to expect. People were everywhere, there didn't appear to be any damage until they turned the corner and could see the picture house had taken a hit. 'Think we had a lucky escape Lizzie, said Bill quietly, 'Can't say the same for the poor beggars that were inside though.' He put his arm around Lizzie's shoulder and pulled her closer to him, 'Come on, let's go for a drink, think we need one.'

Sat in the Kings Head public house with their half pints of beer, they talked, and talked, and talked. Bill told Lizzie about his home, a small Welsh village at the foot of the mountains, the mining community, the snow in winter and the walks amongst the gorse and wildflowers on the Welsh mountains in Summer. All with the promise that he would take her there after the war. Lizzie told Bill about life in Folkestone, her job as a clippie and how she was an only child, adored by her parents. All too soon the evening was at an end, and Bill had to be back in barracks by ten thirty. They said their goodnights after Lizzie assured him that she was happy to take the ten-minute walk home, alone. It was something she was used to.

Lizzie's thoughts were interrupted by a nurse coming into her room. 'Can I get you anything Lizzie?'Asked the young nurse.Lizzie refused the offer of anything, and the nurse closed the door quietly leaving Lizzie with her thoughts.

It was over a week since Lizzie had seen Bill. She knew he had been on several night raids and was on alert for more. Her best friend Flo was able to keep Lizzie informed because she and Jim had become quite an item, and he, as an aircraft mechanic and not flying, was able to pass messages from Bill to Lizzie, via Flo. It was Monday 6th September when Flo went to Lizzie's house. Lizzie had the day off and was helping her mother in the garden. They were digging up potatoes and carrots to go into the vegetable stew. That would be their evening meal. Lizzie could see immediately that Flo was upset.

'Whatever's the matter, Flo?' Asked Lizzie. 'Oh Flo, has

something happened to Jim?' With tears streaming down her cheeks, Flo sobbed out the words. 'No Lizzie, it isn't Jim, it's Bill. I am so sorry.' Lizzie didn't react for a few moments, but then asked, 'Is he dead?' Flo shook her head. 'So he's missing?' Lizzie felt her heart beating rapidly. 'No Lizzie, he isn't missing, his Spitfire was hit and caught fire, Bill bailed out, but he was badly burned.' Flo carried on sobbing. Lizzie felt her legs give way.

Every day for weeks Lizzie borrowed her mum's bicycle and cycled the two miles to RAF Hawkinge where Bill had been stationed. She begged them to tell her something, anything, about Bills condition, his whereabouts. All to no avail. Bill had given strict instructions that if Miss Lizzie Baines came asking after him, she must be told nothing. Bill knew from the moment he set eyes on Lizzie that he loved her, there would never be another girl for him. Now, he was horrifically scarred from his burns, he was blind, and his hands were twisted, fingers webbed together. Better that Lizzie never knew any of this, if she thought of him at all, it would at least be as he was before he was injured.

Lizzie finally gave up her daily cycle to the airfield. Life carried on for her, but she had lost her sparkle. It wasn't all she lost. She had lost her heart to Bill Jenkins. There would be no one else for Lizzie. If she couldn't have her Welshman, she wanted no one.

Finally, the war ended, and Lizzie, like everyone else, celebrated. There was singing and dancing in the streets and life was eventually going to get back to normal. Throughout all of the revelry, Bill was never far from her thoughts. Walking home from her shift one evening Lizzie decided to stop off for a bag of chips, she had been tempted by the delicious aroma permeating the air. 'Bag of chips please.'Lizzie said, 'Lots of salt and vinegar'. The chips were wrapped tightly in newspaper and handed to Lizzie in exchange for her tuppence. Lizzie stepped outside the chip shop and immediately began to unwrap her chips. Taking one out, she blew on it before popping in her mouth. The chips were freshly cooked and very hot. Lizzie was nearly home and decided to throw her chip paper in the dustbin in the garden. There was no litter bin in the street.

Walking through the garden gate Lizzie started to screw the greasy paper up to throw in the bin, but something written in the newspaper caught her eye. Instead of throwing the paper away she took it indoors, went straight into the kitchen and placed it on the kitchen table. Lizzie sat down at the table and smoothed out the chip paper. She began reading the article that caught her eye. PIONEERING NEW TREATMENT FOR BURNS VICTIMS. New Zealander Archibald McIndoe has been practising new techniques for treating burns victims. Primarily, pilots who were severely burned in World War Two.

The article went on to say that the airmen were members of the Guinea Pig Club because that is precisely what they were. These treatments and procedures hadn't been tried before, so the burns victims were, in effect guinea pigs. The article also said that this had been started in 1941.

Lizzie decided that tomorrow she would start searching for Bill via the Guinea Pig Club. For the first time in a very long time, she felt she may actually get somewhere. Lizzie was up bright and early the next morning. Her shift didn't start till midday, so she had a few hours to begin her search. The first place Lizzie went to was the local newspaper office, it was the local paper after all who had published the article. They may have something that could help Lizzie in her quest to find Bill.

The editor of the paper came and spoke to Lizzie, and he listened sympathetically to her story. He didn't think there was anything he could do to help her, after all, everything had been printed in the paper there was nothing else to be added. Disheartened, Lizzie left the building. She hadn't gone too far down the street when she heard someone call out. 'Miss, miss.' Lizzie turned, and a young man said, 'Sorry for shouting out at you down the street miss, but the boss asked me to give you this.' He handed Lizzie a piece of paper with two names on it and a telephone number. 'Boss says if anyone might know, then they might.' Lizzie thanked the young man and looked for the nearest telephone box.

Lizzie entered the phone box and looked at the piece of paper in her hand. Could this slip of paper be the answer to her prayers she wondered? Lizzie picked up the telephone, put it to her ear, then placed her finger in the telephone dial and dialled zero for the operator. 'Good morning caller, number please.' Lizzie hesitated. 'Number please caller' the disembodied voice repeated, sounding a little impatient. Lizzie apologised and gave the operator the information she required. 'Connecting you now caller.'

Lizzie listened to the clicking sound as the operator tried to connect her. Finally, the telephone began to ring out. 'Hello, how may I help you?' It was a well-spoken voice. 'Hello,' Lizzie spoke softly, 'Am I speaking to Mrs Blond?'

'You are indeed dear, what can I do for you?' Lizzie found herself telling Mrs Blond her sad story down to the very last detail. Mrs Blond had listened very carefully to Lizzie. 'Oh dear,' said Mrs Blond sympathetically. 'I am not sure I can help you if our boys don't want loved ones to see them, and many don't, then I am duty bound to say nothing. I really don't think I have any information that will help you.' Lizzie started to weep quietly. 'My dear girl, give me your address. I will look into it for you.' Mrs Blond was moved by Lizzie's obvious distress. 'I can promise you nothing, I can only promise to try.' Lizzie dried her eyes as she told Mrs Blond her address and then thanked her.

Elaine Blond and her husband Neville were good friends of the pioneering surgeon Archibald McIndoe. When the injured airmen were discharged from the hospital, usually many months after their accident, the Blonds opened the door of their home and offered convalescence to the men and helped with reintegration back into normal life. It was in this environment that these young men could be themselves, laugh, joke, drink, and, be rowdy in general. Life for them was normal here. The days that followed Lizzie's telephone conversation with Mrs Blond seemed long and slow-moving to Lizzie. Every morning she would watch out for the postman hoping for news of Bill. Finally, that day arrived, and Lizzie, once again, found herself sitting at the kitchen table, not with a piece of greasy chip paper, but a crisp white envelope addressed to her in impeccable handwriting. 'Dear Miss Baines, I have managed to track down Aircraftman Bill Jenkins. Sadly, I have to inform you that he is still adamant that you shall not visit him. He asks that you respect his wishes. I am so sorry Miss Baines, but it seems your young man has made his mind up. I can, however, inform you that he is well, but still faces a lot of medical treatment, and has adjusted to his situation. Yours most sincerely Elaine Blond.

Lizzie placed the letter on the table and let the tears roll silently down her cheeks. She could do no more. Bill was gone from her forever. She picked up the letter and folded it in half to replace it back in the envelope. On the reverse side of the message was a postscript, though not in the neat handwriting of the letter writer herself. It was an address.

Two weeks later, having taken a weeks holiday from her job, Lizzie found herself outside a house on the outskirts of the village of Kingsclere. She had travelled the eight miles from Basingstoke by taxicab. Lizzie was booked into a single room in a small private hotel in Basingstoke. Flo had an aunt who had lived there and had recommended it to Lizzie, informing her that it was cheap, clean and the food was excellent. Flo had wanted to go with her friend, stating, 'You don't know who wrote the address, Liz, it might not be safe, You shouldn't go alone.' Lizzie was having none of it. She was going alone.

Now she stood alone outside the very address she'd been given, and she wasn't sure what to do next. Any decision she may have made was very soon put to one side as voices coming from the garden made Lizzie step back out of view. There seemed to be a lot of hilarity. Two men laughing and joking. Lizzie leaned forward enough to see the men, what she saw made her gasp. Their features were distorted, they were bearing the scars of very badly burned men. 'Come on you two ne'er do wells, it's almost lunchtime. You have time for one cigarette.' The voice had come from someone who looked like a school matron but was smiling like a doting grandmother. 'Don't be too long.' 'Yes, sir.' One of the men laughed as he spoke. There was no mistaking that beautiful Welsh accent. Lizzie had found her Bill. Lizzie was now able to resume her life in a more relaxed fashion. She knew and accepted that she and Bill would never be together, but he was as happy as he could be and he was getting the care he needed.

Once a year Lizzie took a weeks holiday in Basingstoke and made her way to 'Bills Village'. Sometimes she would see him sitting quietly by himself in the garden. She wondered if he might be thinking of her, or had the tides of time wiped her from his memory. At other times he would be laughing and joking with others, who, like himself, had virtually shunned the outside world because of the way they looked.

Amongst Lizzie's memories, one visit stood out. She heard Bill singing. It was a sunny Sunday afternoon, and the local vicar was making one of his regular visits. Lizzie had seen him pop by on many occasions from the corner of the road where she always watched for Bill. Cwm Rhondda (Guide Me O Thy Great Redeemer) rang out. Lizzie listened and cried. The sound was beautiful to hear. She cried then, as she would cry many more times throughout her life for her lost love. Lizzie continued to make her annual visits until she was too old to do so, and now, as she lay dying in her hospital bed, she thought once more of her lost love. 'Lizzie, it's time to go.' Bill held out his hand. Lizzie rose from her bed and reached out for Bill. Hand in hand they went through the door and onto the Welsh mountain where they would walk amongst the gorse and wildflowers together, for eternity, forever young, and Bill, the handsome young airman once more.

So Lonely

The man sat by the window, just looking out, he looked out at a world he didn't feel part of. Oh, he'd done everything everyone else did. Played in the street as a boy, watched the girls go by as a teen, and finally met, and married the girl of his dreams, but something eluded him. Something stopped him from finding joy in living. The overwhelming feeling throughout his life had been a feeling of loneliness and sadness.

Life for Sean Dooley had been tough. Taken as a young boy from his beloved Ireland where his surroundings were green hills, lush countryside and mountains, to a city in England with buildings close by, no fields to play in, and where he knew only his brothers and sisters, his mum and his dad. He would never know if life may have been different if he had grown up in his homeland. He only knew that his life felt a little more like it should whenever he went home to Ireland.

As the years passed, he struggled with every day living. He was painfully shy. He hated school and found it hard to make friends. He worked because he needed to earn. Few jobs gave him the feeling of a job well done. Work was a necessary evil in his life. A chore to be endured. A life to be endured.

In his mid-teens, he met the girl who was to become his wife. Christine Simms was a dark haired beauty who finally brought some happiness into Sean's life. He never knew where he found the courage to chat to her, and, to finally ask her out on a date because his shyness always prevented him from interacting with others. On that occasion though, the stars must have aligned because everything turned out as he had hoped it would. Christine agreed to be his girl. They dated, became engaged, then the marriage of course followed.

They had two children, first a boy, then, a girl a couple of years later. Sean went through the motions of being a happy family man. He was a good husband and father. He kept a roof over their heads and food on their table. He attended parents evenings at school, accompanied Christine to the school nativities and other social events, but throughout, even when surrounded by people, he still felt dreadful loneliness. It never left him, it lived inside him like a cancer that could not be removed.

As the children grew older, so did the distance between Sean and his offspring. They had no knowledge of how their father felt, how he lived his life on the outside of happiness, looking in at others and wishing he could be the one laughing and joking with his kids in the park. Instead, they didn't go to the park, and they would moan to Christine, asking why their dad wasn't like other dads. She tried to explain that Dad was tired, Dad was feeling a bit sad today. How could she explain Sean's depression to her children, when she couldn't fully understand it herself.

Christine did try to understand it. She went with Sean to his doctor's appointments. Listened when he explained about chemical imbalances in Sean's brain. Watched as yet another prescription for antidepressants was written out. Eventually, she stopped going with him. When summer came, their annual holiday was taken in Ireland. Sean became more animated, more relaxed. He was home, and home was where he was as close to happy as he could be.

The holidays always ended too soon. Goodbyes had to be repeated, and the long trip back to reality began. School for the children, and work for Sean beckoned. Finally, the children went off to college, spent less and less time at home and Sean and Christine spent the evenings quietly watching television. They rarely went out socially, and when they did, Sean made an effort to talk to friends and family, but his heart was never really in it. It was on these occasions that Sean wondered how he could still feel so lonely surrounded by people, people who cared about him.

The years passed, Sean and Christine became grandparents to their daughter's only son, but distance decreed they saw little of their grandson. His parents emigrated to New Zealand just after he was born. They travelled back a couple of times, but work commitments and expense prevented too many visits.

This state of affairs was hard for Sean and Christine. They would have enjoyed getting to know their young grandson, especially realising that their son wanted no children at all, this youngster was going to be the only one. More difficult for Christine of course, she would have spent a lot of time with the boy, Sean would have done his best, but his best was becoming harder to achieve. The less time he spent with others, the more he realised he didn't want to.

Eventually, Christine stopped trying to persuade Sean to go out socially. She would meet friends for a meal out, or visit their homes for coffee, he stayed home with his thoughts. Then came retirement. The days were long and quiet. They had regular shopping days, attended the odd medical appointment when needed. Really only going out if essential.

Their son visited from time to time, sometimes with a girlfriend in tow. Sean couldn't keep up with his son's lifestyle, but it was his life. They had very little to say to each other. Their daughter rang a couple of times a month. Sean always chatted to her for a few minutes, and he enjoyed hearing about his grandson's progress in school, but still happy to pass the phone back to Christine.

Sean, having lived with this dark cloud hanging over him his whole life, thought he could never feel any worse. Sadly, that proved to be untrue. When he lost Christine to a sudden and cruel illness, he plunged into the depths of his depression. No one could reach him. Both his son and daughter tried, other friends and family reached out to him. The loneliness enveloped him. Could he ever be free he wondered?

Sean had been on his own for two years, and as he sat by the window, looking out, he hoped today he would find a little joy in his life. His grandson, now aged nineteen years, had opted to take a gap year. His studies would keep. Today was the day he was arriving, to spend time getting to know the granddad he barely knew. They were even taking a trip to Ireland, for Sean to show his grandson the place he still called home.

As Sean sat, watching, and waiting, he reflected back on his life. He always knew he was surrounded by love, but this wretched, invisible illness called depression had prevented him enjoying it. He knew that his grandson's visit wasn't a cure-all, he would still feel lonely and sad at times, but he would make an effort, he was actually looking forward to his visit. Sean could see a tall, dark-haired young man walking down the street, a rucksack on his back. He was here. Sean got up from his chair and went to open the door to welcome his guest. He was smiling.

Them and Us

The church is packed. I bet the vicar wishes his congregation was this big on a Sunday. Amazing just how many turn up to church for a wedding. Of course, there's them on the one side, and us on the other. There seems more of them than us. I was told to keep numbers down to a minimum. Obviously so they could have more of their side at the wedding. Typical. I have lost count of how many of my family I have offended by not inviting them.Great Aunt Rose for one, and I am very fond of her. She's in her dotage, and a crazy old coot, wish I'd invited her now. She would have livened up proceedings.

My boys have scrubbed up well. They both look rather handsome in their wedding attire. Groom and best man, twin brothers, dressed the same for the first time in twenty years, excluding school uniforms of course. Seeing them standing there now, side by side, wearing matching navy blue suits (her choice) and pale blue waistcoats, ties, and of course, pocket handkerchiefs. (I think I would have preferred white shirts instead of pale blue though.) I feel quite emotional.

She is already fashionably late, people are getting restless. It was stipulated very early on that there would be no children at the wedding, (there's a few more offended). As she is late, it's probably just as well that children were excluded, they would be sliding up the aisles of the church on their knees by now.

The music is depressing, rather dirge-like. Almost like funeral music. The flowers are very pretty though, all cream and pink, rosebuds and carnations. Her mother has just come in, the bridesmaids must be here.

She's a funny woman. Twittery somehow. She's dressed in a lemon two-piece,. It's shiny. Not too sure about the hat. The style probably has a name. To me, it looks somewhat like a pudding basin. Its black, and is sporting a yellow feather. A black clutch bag and black court shoes complete her ensemble. Oh, hang on, The Wedding March. Think we are finally ready for the main event.

She's twenty minutes late. My boys shuffle into place, bless them. We all stand, I have to turn and take a look at the young woman who is to become my daughter in law. She looks stunning. I imagined she'd go for the 'meringue' look, but no, she is wearing a very sleek, fitted dress. It seems quite plain until she gets closer to me and I can see the whole dress is covered in delicate embroidery. The dress is ivory in colour, and quite, quite, exquisite. Her long blonde hair is styled in a simple chignon and caught up in a beaded, open lace snood. She is not overly tall, so she has opted for plain, off-white sandals with a heel. She is carrying two long-stemmed roses. One cream and one pink. The stems are bound with pale blue and navy blue ribbons. She has walked down the aisle on the arm of her father. He, of course, dressed in the same attire as my boys, looks very proud, and rightly so. The bridesmaids followed her up the aisle. Her sister and her best friend. Both pretty girls.They are wearing A-Line, knee length, chiffon dresses. One in pale pink, the other in cream. The dresses have scoop necklines, lace bodices, and satin sashes at the waist. Both girls are wearing strappy sandals that match their dress colours, and they are carrying posies of cream and pink carnations. Their long hair has been left loose and gently curled, giving a very natural look. The Vicar has just stepped forward.

'We are gathered here together in the sight of God'......... It was a nice service, but they took ages in the Vestry signing the register. No matter, we are outside St Caspian's church now. A few photographs are taken here, then on to the reception. That's being held in a Social Club.

The photographer is a bit of a faffer, I do wish he'd hurry up.

These shoes are killing my feet. I knew I should have gone for something flatter. They do make a beautiful couple. I'm still not sure about her mother's suit though, that shiny material isn't flattering.

We are all in the venue now, for the reception. More photos have been taken, inside and out. The room looks charming. Pink and cream balloons, yet more pink and cream flowers and lovely pale, and navy blue ribbons. Everything very nicely colour coordinated.

I was hoping for a 'sit down' meal, but it looks like it's going to be a buffet, or, as I prefer to call it, a, 'get in quick, it won't last long,' meal. It's still them and us, and there's still more of them than us.

We are all sitting on one side of the room, they are on the other side. That's the problem with a buffet, no seating plan needed because there are no set tables, except there does seem to be a top table. I have just glanced up and noticed the ceiling is swathed in cream and pink drapes, much the same as you see in the big marquees. Wonder why they didn't just go for the big marquee.

I have just been dragged...Okay, escorted, to the top table. Think I get to sit between my boys. Perfect. Joy of joys, we also get our buffet brought to us. I have a marvellous view of them and us from here.

I can see that Cousin Jean is sitting as far away from Cousin Bill as possible. They fell out last Christmas and haven't spoken since. Elaine and Derek are gazing into each other's eyes. Talk about loves young dream. They have been married twenty years, wouldn't you think they would have got past the dewy-eyed looks by now. Apparently not.

I did think my boy's father might turn up, but he hasn't so far. He hasn't really bothered with them since they were small. The odd Christmas card with a fiver in it. Just the one card, and the one fiver. Don't know if he forgot he had twins, or if he was just very mean. He had evidently forgotten their birth date because he has never acknowledged their birthdays. Not since the day, he walked out on us, announcing he didn't want to be a husband or a dad, anymore.

Over on the 'them' side, things look a little tense. I think it might be handbags at dawn between the two grandmothers. They are wearing the same hat, silver grey cloche type. Oh dear. Their outfits aren't dissimilar either. Obviously no pre-wedding outfit discussion between those two. I don't think the grandmothers are as old as my mother, but they are dressed somewhat grandmotherly. I glance over at my own mother, she waves at me, big beam on her face. She couldn't be more different if she tried. Long multicoloured dress, kimono style jacket, casually draped over her shoulders, her ever-present beads, her turquoise hair, cut and styled in a bob, and those ruddy Doc Marten boots that I begged her not to wear. That's my mother, and the boys adore her. I know that she too has noticed the tension on the opposing side, the look she gives me tells me so.

The speeches are taking forever. I'm surprised they haven't heard my stomach rumbling. The adverts can say what they like, but those breakfast biscuits do NOT fill you like a full English. Going back to the speeches, I couldn't help but notice her fathers shoulders. Navy blue and dandruff, not a good combination. Reminded me I must get the door frame painted around the front door. Every time I slam the door shut, a bit more paint falls to the floor in little flakes.

I think its nearly time for the food. The cake is being cut afterwards I believe. It looks as though there is some form of service. Two young men have just stepped behind the buffet table, so it is being served, but still has to be queued for. Top table has been waited on. Pretty run of the mill fare really. Cold chicken, ham, mixed salads, quiche, and a few veggie options. Caramelised onion tartlets, savoury eggs and some tofu concoction. No one has said if there is to be any entertainment later, but quite honestly, if there is, it won't better what we have just had. Someone dropped a slice of ham on the floor, it sat there, quite inconspicuously, waiting to be trodden on, (which of course it was), by my new daughter-in-law's grandmother. She skidded across the room at the speed of light, trying to stay upright. Two brave souls tried to work out which way she might go down so they could catch her. She went in the opposite direction to them. As she landed, her hat slipped over one ear, and her right arm and leg went skywards. Her plate of food was catapulted through the air, and vegetable missiles went in every direction. I didn't think you could still buy those knickers with the legs and elasticated bottoms, but you apparently can. Hers were dusky pink. At least she hadn't gone commando! I didn't look across at my mother or anyone else for that matter. I didn't dare.

The two who had hoped to catch her, and failed, helped her up. One attempted to straighten her hat from its jaunty angle, while the other brushed her down. Those still in the buffet queue were busy removing bits of greenery and tomato pips from their wedding finery. One woman had a cherry tomato caught firmly between the two large flowers on her hat. It added a splash of colour. Grandma was okay. A bit shaken up but a large brandy sorted her out.

I expected something sweet to follow the savoury offerings, but it seems the Wedding Cake is doubling up as dessert. A bit of cost-cutting there methinks. It's a good looking cake. Three, no, four tiers. The decoration is simple but very effective. The royal icing is pink and cream and has been swirled on, blending the two colours. It looks somewhat like marble. Very pretty! In the four corners of each of the four tiers are small pink and cream rosebuds that have been modelled from tragacanth icing. In the centre of the top tier, there is a little spray of cream and pink rosebuds and carnations, again, fashioned from icing. The flowers are very lifelike! My daughter in laws mother has just informed me we have a choice of cake. Each tier is apparently different. Fruit, chocolate, jam and cream or coconut. Nothing like catering for all. Think I will stick with the fruitcake. Seems a shame to cut it, but they are going for it.

It was a nice cake. Cannot vouch for any of the other flavours, but the fruitcake was rich, moist, spicy, and full of fruit. Also had a good layer of marzipan between the icing and the cake. Lovely.

The DJ arrived a short while ago. He's been busy setting up his equipment. I do hope he doesn't play too much of the modern stuff, I can't be doing with it. A bit of easy listening that would be perfect.

I have noticed there seems to be a little less them and us. I do believe there is a bit of mingling going on. My cousin Davina has been batting her eyes at some silver-haired chap who wandered over to her from the 'them' side. He's gay apparently. I daresay she will realise soon enough. Probably when he gets up to dance with his partner. She's not very quick off the mark. My mother has started tapping her Doc Martens to the beat of the music. Another couple of Vodkas and she'll be tripping the light fantastic around the floor like a demented Ginger Rogers. Heaven help the poor fellow who she sets her sights on as her Fred. Refusal is futile, I've seen her in action.

There seem to be a few more bodies drifting in. The second wave of guests are coming in for the evening do. Well, the disco anyway. The DJ has just announced that the Bride and Groom will be dancing the first dance in a few moments. Their chosen music is, Love Is All Around. It's the Wet Wet Wet version. Personally, I would have gone for The Troggs. Still a lovely song though, and perfect for the occasion. As the music rings out, and as my son and daughter-in-law glide across the floor in each other's arms I look around.

We may have been them and us at the beginning of the day, but now, watching everyone, chatting, dancing, drinking and laughing together, I do believe we have the makings of a lovely family. I'm still not too sure about that shiny, lemon two-piece though!

The Great Outdoors

The wind howled, and the rain lashed down. The two girls huddled together, more from fear than for warmth. The noise from the rain hitting the canvas tent was like nothing they had heard before. 'Don't touch the canvas,' shouted Tammy. 'If you do the tent will leak and we'll be soaked.' 'I can barely move,' shouted Jo, above the noise of the rain. 'This tent was never intended to house any more than us two and our sleeping bags. Look, we are sharing with two bulging rucksacks, two collapsible chairs, a small camping stove and two pairs of hiking boots.' Tammy shone her torch around the tent. 'Yes, you are right,' she laughed, then asked 'Are we mad?'. 'Probably,' giggled Jo,'But it will be fun if it ever stops raining.'

The two girls had been friends since infant school and were inseparable. Now aged nineteen, they were getting prepared to go to university. For the first time, they would not be sitting side by side to do their studying. They had picked different universities. Tammy was going to become a medical student and had secured a place at Imperial College, London. Jo was heading for Swansea University in South Wales to study Zoology. Both of them excelled at school and had worked diligently to gain the required 'A' Level results to ensure they could each follow their chosen career path. This short camping trip was their last hurrah before they knuckled down to some seriously hard work.

Both girls were fond of the great outdoors having been brought up with families who believed that fresh air, a good walk and getting 'out there' was the cure for all ills. 'I suppose we should try to sleep,' yelled Jo, 'and let's hope the rain subsides a little'. Both girls slipped further down their sleeping bags and shouted goodnight to each other before pulling their sleeping bags over their heads, in the hope it may drown out the sound of the rain. Surprisingly, the two girls slept and awoke to feel refreshed.

The sun was shining, the rain had stopped, and the birds were singing from their perches high up in the surrounding conifer trees. They dressed and took their little camping stove just outside the tent. Bottled water was poured into the small billy-can and placed on the stove to boil. A nice brew and they would hike to the nearest village for breakfast.

The two girls decided not to move on, but to spend another night hoping that today's sun would help dry the tent. They certainly didn't want to pack away a wet tent. They removed from their rucksacks all that they needed for a lazy amble around the countryside. Waterproofs, compasses and the map. They each had small, lightweight backpacks to use when just out on a ramble and these were easily tucked away in their rucksacks when not in use.

Once ready for the off the friends checked that all of their belongings were inside the small tent which they then closed. 'I'm starving,'said Tammy, 'It seems ages since we had those cheese baguettes, we must remember to get some chocolate today. It will come in handy if we get the munchies.'

'Good idea Tams, and some biscuits. There will be plenty of time to worry about our diets later, 'stated Jo, 'For now though, let's just have a great time and eat what we want, when we want.'

Tammy and Jo set off on their ramble to the village of Lower Mulberry where they would hopefully find a cafe or tea room where they could eat. It would only take about thirty minutes to reach the village, and over breakfast, they would decide where they were going, and what they would be doing for the remainder of the day.

While walking to the village, the two girls excitedly discussed their futures, listened to the birdsong, and admired the changing colours in the trees. It was the beginning of September, and it looked like Autumn could come early this year. The end of the month would see them entering the new phase in their lives, and they could hardly wait.

When they arrived, they began to look for a place to eat. The two girls wandered past a row of thatched cottages with gardens still pretty and colourful with summer blooms, resplendent in the late summer sun. Part way up the road was a picturesque church, and leaning against the Lych gate was a young man. He didn't seem to be doing much, just leaning. 'Excuse me,' said Tammy. 'You couldn't tell us if there is a cafe in the village could you!' The young man looked the two girls up and down, then smiled. 'Yep, just walk to the end of this road.' He said and pointed towards the top of the lane. 'If you turn left you will find the thriving High Street of Lower Mulberry. There is a Post Office, a bakery and a pub.' There was more than a hint of irony in his tone. 'The Post Office doubles up with the supermarket, and the bakery has a cafe on the side.' He finished his short introduction to Lower Mulberry with, 'Oh yes, we have it all here.'

They thanked him for his help and carried on walking up the road past yet more little cottages. They both agreed that the young man didn't appear totally enamoured with his village. Two minutes later the girls found themselves in the High Street. There weren't many people about. Tammy and Jo followed their noses to the bakery. The mouthwatering smell of bread baking was wafting down the street, it reminded the two that they were hungry, and more than ready to eat.

The sign above the shop window said Cosy Cafe and Bakery. The contents displayed in the window looked very inviting. Jo pushed open the little shop door, and as she, and then Tammy, stepped inside the aromatic bakery, a small bell tinkled above their head. Obviously alerting assistants to customers entering the establishment. 'Won't keep you a moment,' someone shouted. The two girls looked around but couldn't work out where the voice had come from. Suddenly an elderly lady popped up from behind the counter, rather like a Jack In The Box. 'Ooh, sorry to keep you,' she said but offered no explanation as to why she had been out of view and, presumably, on the floor. Jo and Tammy looked at each other trying very hard not to laugh, but not quite managing it. 'Now then girls, what can I do for you?' The old lady said.

The girls found themselves sitting at a little round table with a lemon and white gingham tablecloth. The cafeteria was situated on the side of the bakery and was reached by going through a beaded curtain just opposite the counter. It was barely noticeable on entering the shop, and the two girls had to be shown where to go. They had studied the somewhat limited menu, and both decided a bacon sandwich would go down well with a pot of tea. While they waited, they decided they would like to go and have a look around the local supermarket and see what provisions they may need, not forgetting the all-important chocolate and biscuits. They also agreed that a wander around the pretty little church they passed on the way to the cafe would be nice, and maybe a look around the churchyard.

Soon their food arrived, and they tucked in hungrily. Once the sandwiches had been devoured and the teapot drained, Tammy and Jo left the cafe and headed to the building with the Post Office sign hanging above it. They knew that was where they would find the supermarket. Once again, the tinkling of the bell above the door announced their arrival. The 'supermarket' was more village shop but seemed to offer a varied choice. Tammy headed straight to the sweet section and picked up two family-sized bars of milk chocolate, while Jo searched for the chocolate digestives.

'Do we need anything else Jo?' Tammy queried as she

studied the shelves. 'No, I don't think so Tams,' responded Jo. 'We have those pot noodle things for tonight, we have crisps, and we are okay for coffee and dried milk.' She too then began looking at the food shelves, just in case something sprang to mind. 'Water,' shouted Jo, making Tammy jump. 'Think we had better take a two-litre bottle back, we don't want to run out.'

Goodies paid for, the two girls left the shop. Once outside it was noticeably duller. The sun had disappeared, and it looked like the rain clouds were gathering again. 'Oh no, not more rain,' sighed Tammy. 'What do you think Jo? Shall we have a quick look around the churchyard and then head back. Maybe have a quiet afternoon, we can play Travel Scrabble.' Jo agreed it was a good idea, and they headed off in the direction of the church.

They entered the churchyard via the Lytch gate where they had asked the young man for directions. He was nowhere to be seen. It was a neat churchyard, and the graves were well tended. The grass was short, and it was easy to wander amongst the tombs to read names and epitaphs on the gravestones. The first spots of rain started to fall, and both girls simultaneously reached inside their backpacks and pulled out their waterproof jackets. 'Think it's time to go,' said Jo. 'Maybe we could come back tomorrow and see the inside of the church.' Tammy agreed. They walked briskly away from the little churchyard in the vain hope they could reach their campsite before they got too wet.

Once back at the tent, the waterproofs were removed and placed where they could not make anything else wet.. The tent flaps were left open, and the camping stove lit. A cup of coffee, chocolate biscuits and a game of Scrabble -what could be more relaxing? As evening approached Tammy and Jo discussed their plans for the following day. They both agreed that the church at Lower Mulberry was worth another visit, and hopefully inside the church this time.

The rain was still falling steadily, but nothing like it had been the previous night, and no howling wind either.. When nightfall arrived, the girls were already snuggled up in their sleeping bags. They had played Scrabble, read their books, eaten their noodles and devoured a whole block of chocolate. 'We will need to do a ten-mile hike tomorrow Jo.' Tammy was laughing as she said it.

'We will need to walk off the calories.' 'Oh no,' was Jo's response. 'Eight should do it.' Both girls said goodnight to each other, still laughing. 'Jo, you did turn the camping stove off properly didn't you? You know how the switch sticks sometimes. Tammy sounded a little worried. 'Yes,' said Jo. 'I am sure I did.' Both girls closed their eyes and were lulled gently to sleep by the rain. They didn't hear the creaking of the big conifer that was towering above them. By the time they did, the conifer was falling, its shallow roots loosened and uprooted from the sodden ground. No one heard their screams as the unforgiving tree crashed down upon their tent. As in life, in death, they were also inseparable.

The Petty Thief

David crept quietly along the dark avenue. It was 3 00 a.m., and the street lamps offered a very moribund light. There was no moon, and the sky was black and heavy. Storm clouds had been gathering all day, it looked as though the thunder could be his enemy tonight.

David Benton had two jobs. By day he was a much-loved children's entertainer. By night he was a petty thief. He loved his day job, but it was poorly paid. At 53 years of age, he was never going to make the big time. So in the wee small hours, David eked out his meagre income by petty thieving. David didn't go out every night, and he never ever took from people who couldn't afford to 'lose' anything.

The first rumble of thunder came just as David turned out of the avenue and onto the canal towpath. David hoped there wouldn't be too much lightning, he didn't need extra light and certainly didn't need sleeping victims to be disturbed by a violent storm. His extra night time activities demanded darkness, and preferably, silence.

The house he had chosen to rob tonight was at the other end of the towpath, but as the house in question was almost reached, David saw a very bright flash of lightning and heard a yell, followed by a splash. He ran to where he thought the yell had come from. 'Help me, I can't swim.' A man's voice called out in the darkness. David jumped into the murky canal, not giving a single thought for his own safety. He swam around, shouting, 'Where are you? Where are you? I can't see you'. David kept reaching out trying to find the man, he had to be here.

After what seemed like forever, David felt a jacket, he pulled it towards him, feeling relieved that there was someone inside it. He made his way to the side of the canal with the man, pushed him, half drowned, out of the water, and then heaved himself out. David lay on his back on the ground gasping for air. That had been very strenuous, and far more exercise than he had attempted in a very long time. 'Thank you,' said a quiet voice. David sat up and saw a man sitting on a bench. The man was dry, surely he wasn't the one who had just been saved from drowning, but even in the poor light, David could see there was no one else there.

David stood up and joined the man on the bench. They sat side by side in silence for a short while. Then the man spoke. 'You are basically a decent man David Benton, so,' he asked. 'Why do you steal?' David found himself telling the stranger that he loved his day job entertaining the children with his silly magic tricks and his talking cuddly toys. But it hardly paid the bills. A few birthday parties, the odd Nursery visit. It was never enough. To help him get by, David explained that he 'visited' the houses he had entertained in. He never took money or valuables. Just food. 'Food!' The man seemed surprised by this revelation. 'Yes, food,' Said David. 'It saves me buying it, and I see the waste when I do my entertaining. The party food that goes in the bin, the buffets that mums can't eat because they are watching their weight. They probably don't even miss what I take from their food store. The odd ready meal from the fridge, a couple of sausages, a few slices of bread. I am never greedy sir, I only take what I can eat'. The stranger smiled. 'You will be fine David. Good things happen to good people.'

'Tell me something,' David turned towards the stranger as he spoke. 'How do you know my name?' There was no one there. David looked around him. He shivered, but not from the cold, wet clothes. He was no longer wet. The sky was lighter now, dawn was breaking. The storm came to nothing, but it was too late for petty thieving. David made his way home.

He opened his front door, and there was a handwritten note

on the mat. One single sheet of paper folded in half. All it said was David Benton ring this number. He rang the number immediately, and a voice answered before the second ring. 'Hello,' David began.

'Ah, Mr Benton, I have been expecting your call. I believe you can help me. I am in desperate need of a children's entertainer. I have it on good authority that you are the best. It's a full-time position. Will you take up the job?'

'Well yes,' answered a puzzled David, 'Of course I will, but where is the job? Who will I be working for? Do I know you?' The voice on the end of the phoned laughed. 'I own a toy shop Mr Benton, children from nine months to ninety years come in daily. I like to offer a little more than just a browse. I think you are just what my shop needs. I'll be in touch.'

The line went dead. As David put his phone down, he felt confident he knew the voice of the toy shop owner, but couldn't think who he was, or, how he might know him. He smiled, it didn't really matter. Suddenly life began to look up, and David somehow knew that from today onwards, life would not be quite the same.

One Christmas Eve

The young man stood and watched as people went about their business. He smiled to himself. Pushing and shoving, jostling for a place on the pavement, people everywhere. It was Christmas Eve, and last-minute shoppers were dashing in and out of the Christmas bedecked stores in that last desperate hope of finding a much-wanted toy, or that piece of jewellery that should have been bought weeks back, but somehow wasn't. It was cold, and excited children all dressed in their winter hats and scarves were driving mums and dads to distraction.

The young man stepped forward, as he did so he caught his foot on the base of a litter bin he hadn't noticed was there. He lurched forward, and had it not been for the strong arm that grabbed and held onto him, he would have fallen headlong into the busy road at precisely the same time the number 43 bus was passing. 'Phew, thanks mate' said the young man as he looked into the face of an elderly gentleman with kind eyes. 'My pleasure young fellow, can't have you falling under the number 43 on Christmas Eve'.There was laughter in the elderly gents voice.

There was something about him the young man liked, and he heard himself saying,'Have you got time for a cuppa?' The elderly gentleman said he had all the time in the world, and added that there was a cafe across the road. The young man cupped his hand under the elderly gents elbow, and together they ventured forth across the busy road. Safely over, they entered the warm cafe.

'Two coffees please Cath, when you're ready' shouted the older of the two men. 'OK Bill' said Cath, 'Two ticks, and I will bring 'em over.'

'So, you are a regular here,' said the young man. 'Oh, and by the way, my name's Gary, Gary Jamieson, how do you do.' 'How do you do Gary Jamieson' said the elderly gent holding out his hand. 'Bill Wilson at your service.' Gary took Bill's hand, and they shared a firm handshake. Cath came over carrying two mugs of steaming, hot coffee. 'Here we are boys, she said cheerfully, 'Enjoy.'

'So Gary, what are you doing, your Christmas shopping?' Bill asked. Gary laughed and said, 'Yes, as always, last minute. Just chocolates and smellies for my mum. I buy her the same every year, then I help her to eat the chocs.' Bill looked serious for a moment, then spoke. 'But not this year eh Gary.' An anxious Gary queried Bill, 'Oh my God, have I left it too late, has the store shut?' Gary looked out of the cafe window and across the road to the store that was still open. He saw a small gathering of people. 'Wonder what's happening over there' he said. 'It's you' said Bill, 'Don't you remember falling under the wheels of the number 43 bus, you're dead, Gary'.

Although very nervously, Gary laughed. 'What did you say' Bill repeated his previous statement, but Gary only heard two words. You're dead. Gary laughed again. 'No I'm not, I'm sat here having a coffee with you.' He looked up, he was alone. There was no one there, no cafe, no mugs of coffee, no Cath and no Bill. There was nothing but a black abyss.

The Anniversary

Once again the special day had arrived. It seemed to come around sooner and sooner with each passing year. Could it really be a full twelve months, it felt like only yesterday. Angie looked at the cake on the table. She had spent the past week decorating it in pale lemon and white icing. The same colour, year in, year out. Angie couldn't really remember a time when the anniversary hadn't been a part of her life. It had always been a constant. She looked at the cake again, and at the scrolled black lettering, so glaringly stark against the lemon and white icing. R.I.P ANGELO.

Angie reached into her kitchen cupboard and brought out a deep, plastic cake container, she removed the lid and placed the cake inside. She then snapped the lid on tightly and put the container and its contents on the top shelf of her food cupboard. She didn't want to look at it anymore.

As she turned towards the kitchen table, she stepped back with a gasp. Someone was sitting at the table watching her. 'Who the hell are you?' Angie asked even though there was a familiarity about him. She felt she knew him. 'Don't you recognise me?' He smiled a lazy smile at her. Angie stared at the handsome, dark-haired, young man. It was like looking at a mirror image; she knew that face. It was her face. Of course, there were differences. The hint of stubble, the heavier eyebrows, the piercing, deep blue eyes. Hers were hazel. But the face was unmistakable, it was her face. He sneered at her.. 'Oh yes, you recognise me alright. SURPRISE!!!

'Angelo?' Angie asked, while looking at him with the mixed feelings of fear and disbelief. 'But it can't be you, you're dead, you never even lived.'

'And you did,' he said nastily, 'and you have spent your life denying my existence.' Angie shook from head to foot, could this really be happening. Had the anniversary finally taken her to the edge of sanity? She always thought that one day it might. She looked again at the young man. 'Yes, you are right. I have never acknowledged you.' Angie said bitterly because you never existed, yet you still managed to blight my life.' He looked at her and shook his head. 'You have no idea how it's been for me, watching you grow, making friends.' Angelo shouted,

'LIVING YOUR LIFE.' Angie yelled back at him. 'LIVING MY LIFE? I should have been so lucky. I was never allowed to just live my life, Angelo.' 'You say you were watching, then surely you could see that I was never allowed to forget I was a twin. But I wasn't was I? I wasn't a twin because you were stillborn.' Angie started to sob. 'How could you do that to me? Why did you die? Why couldn't you have survived too?' 'Mum and Dad never let me forget that there should have been two of us, every birthday. But it wasn't a birthday for me, it was a memorial for you. It was always about you. The anniversary of your death Angelo, never my birth.'

Angelo stood and walked towards Angie. 'I am so sorry,' he said. 'I was so bitter at having to grow up in the spirit world, I never thought how it might be for you. Please don't cry Angie, you may not know it, but I was there. I was always there.' He looked sadly at Angie. 'I wanted you to see me so often. But I was angry because you denied my ever having been. So much negativity. It was never going to be possible for you to see me.'

'So what has changed now?' Angie asked. 'Why can I see you today?'

'Today is our twenty-first birthday. It should be special Angie. I guess I think it's now or never. I just want you to acknowledge you have a brother.' All anger had left him. The pair were silent for a while, they just stood, facing each other in the kitchen. Angie broke the silence. 'Mum and Dad never got over losing you Angelo, and somehow, I always felt that they would have been happier if you had lived and I had died.' Tears slid down Angie's cheeks as she told Angelo of her misery, and yes, her guilt at being alive. Angelo stepped forward and wrapped his arms around his twin sister. 'But they love you so much Angie, you must know that?'

'Of course I do,' she cried, 'I don't think they even realised how it made me feel every time my birthday came around. I dreaded it. Two cakes, Happy Birthday Angie, R.I.P Angelo. Why do you think they kept doing that Angelo?'

'Because you never asked them to stop Angie, that's why.' Angie looked at her brother incredulously. 'What! Are you telling me that it would all have stopped if I had just asked?' Angie pulled away from her brother and reached for the cake container off the top of the food cupboard. She carried it to the table and placed it down. Removing the lid, she looked at her brother and smiled. She took the cake from the container and fetched a knife from the cutlery drawer. Very carefully Angie scraped the black lettering from the cake. 'No more R.I.P ANGELO.' She delved in her cupboard and brought out a pack of ready-made, and rolled icing. Angelo sat back and watched as his sister deftly cut out letters from the rolled icing using a small knife. 'Your cake icing classes taught you well,' he remarked. Angie looked at him and laughed, ' So you WERE around!'

'Answer me a question' he said. 'Why yellow and white icing?'

'Oh that's an easy one,' Angie replied. 'Mum was convinced we would either be identical boys or identical girls, so, until she got to know who of us was who, we would be dressed one in yellow and the other in white. It never entered her head that she may have one of each.'

'Or that she may have only one,' commented Angelo. Angie frowned, 'I'm so sorry Angelo, I wish it could have been different.' He smiled his lazy smile, and said 'Hey you, don't you have a party to get ready for?'

'Will you be there?' She asked.

Haven't missed one yet.' Angelo replied.

Angie replaced the cake back in its container and returned it to the top of the food cupboard. When she turned her kitchen was empty. There was no one there. 'Angelo?' She whispered, but there was no answer. She sat for a moment wondering if she had been dreaming. No, surely not. It felt too real. She thought.

Two hours later Angie walked into the local Community Centre where she was to celebrate her twenty-first birthday. Her friends and family were all there to help her celebrate. Angie took the cake container to the table and removed the newly decorated cake. She placed it next to the cake also decorated with yellow and white icing, which merely said Happy 21st Birthday Angela. 'Thank you, sis,' whispered Angelo in Angie's ear. 'I love my cake.' It was iced to perfection.

Angie whispered 'Happy 21st Birthday Angelo. You would have been the perfect brother. I love you'.

Angie danced the night away, and for the first time enjoyed the 'anniversary'. She would never see Angelo again, but she knew he was waiting for her, and that he would always watch over her. She had a brother, and she loved him.

Duncan

I sat with my legs dangling over the edge of the bridge. Looking down I could see the white water swirling and seething. Bubbling like some effervescent brew. If I just close my eyes and let myself fall forward, I would have freedom. No more pain or sadness. It would be so easy, and quick.

I started to lean forward, and just as I was about to close my eyes, hopefully for the last time, someone grabbed me and pulled me backwards. I came off the bridge and landed on the pavement in an ungainly sprawl. 'What are you doing?' A very high pitched voice screeched in my ear.

'Let go of me.' I yelled. I would have yelled a lot more had it not been for what was sprawled on the pavement with me, (and still hanging on to me). I was temporarily struck dumb by the sight of a man-sized red squirrel. The squirrel was dressed in a rather fetching, if somewhat dated, flying jacket. On top of his head was a set of headphones. He was never going to benefit from them. The earpieces were on the side of his head, and his ears stood bolt upright on the top of his head above the headphones. 'GET OFF ME YOU OVERSIZED TREE RAT.' I yelled, then pushed the squirrel off me and stood up. Brushing myself down I stared at the squirrel, and said. 'You aren't wearing any trousers.' He'd taken the trouble to dress his top half but just didn't bother with his bottom half.

The red squirrel with the high pitched voice said, as he got up off the ground, 'You don't remember me do you?' I looked at him and stated categorically that I had never clapped eyes on him before. 'I feel pretty confident that had never met a half dressed, man-sized, red squirrel I think I would have remembered. I said.

'But you must remember,' insisted the squirrel, ' You swerved to avoid me last week. I was sat in the middle of the lane trying to remember under which tree I had hidden my acorns. You came speeding along on your bike, saw me, swerved, managed to miss me, and fell off.'

'That wasn't you. The squirrel I avoided was a normal sized little red squirrel. I am sure if you had been sitting there I couldn't possibly have missed you. The lane is far too narrow.'

I was starting to feel very angry. I was also beginning to question my own sanity, (well, I was talking to a half dressed, man-sized squirrel). I had even convinced myself that he wasn't wearing any trousers because his tail got in the way. Though thinking about it, Basil Brush had a tail, and he always managed. Anyway, that's beside the point. I was angry because I was about to throw myself off the bridge until this vermin interrupted. This had been my darkest hour, then Supersquirrel turns up and hey presto, I'm still here, not even remembering why I was about to launch myself off into the churning water.

'If I may just interrupt your reverie for one moment.' The squirrel made me jump, I was far away in my own thoughts. I looked up and saw, not a squirrel standing before me, but a tall, red-headed man sporting a very impressive red beard. He was wearing a flying jacket, headphones and, not trousers, but a kilt..a red tartan. 'I'm sorry,' he said, 'I didn't mean to startle you, but before I go, I wanted to be sure you were okay'.

'Oh, you aren't a squirrel after all.' I think he probably knew he wasn't.

'I beg your pardon, did you say squirrel?' It was now the turn of the bearded one to be puzzled. I smiled and told him for one brief moment, as he was helping me up off the ground, I thought he was a red squirrel.

'Did you bump your head when you fell?' He asked. 'I worried that you were going to fall off the bridge and go hurtling into the water. There should be railings there.'

'No, no bump on the head, and yes, you are right, there should be railings. If you hadn't been walking by as I fell, I think I may have gone into the water. Thank goodness you grabbed my collar. Thank you.'

The bearded one smiled back. 'Just returning the favour, you swerved and avoided hitting me last week when I stepped off the pavement without looking. You were on your bike.' I laughed, and he asked if I fancied a coffee. That was six months ago. Duncan and I have been together ever since. I don't call him Duncan though. I call him Squirrel.

Amphlett

Sid Jones and Barney Sykes glared at each other from opposite ends of the table. Both members of the church committee, they disliked each other immensely. Sid was a very amiable sort of chap. He was a retired thatcher and had lived in the village of Amphlett his whole life. Barney, on the other hand, was a relative newcomer to the village, he and his wife Prudence had only lived there for fifteen years. He referred to himself as a retired Major. It was only days after 'Major' and Mrs Sykes moved into the newly acquired Holly Cottage that hostilities broke out between the two men.

Barney was convinced the thatched roof of his cottage was leaking. On the advice of other villagers, Barney asked Sid if he would check out the cottage roof for him. He had been assured that Sid Jones was the very best thatcher by a country mile. He would have a hard job finding a better thatcher than Sid. Sid was more than willing to oblige.

Sidney Charles Jones was a workman of the old school. When he said, he would be starting a job at 8 30 am. He would be there on the dot, ready to start. Sure enough, at 8 30am on Monday 6th March, Sid turned up at Holly Cottage, the date and time the two men had agreed upon. To the chagrin of Sid, Barney was still enjoying a leisurely breakfast. His wife, a very mousy woman, scurried out with profuse apologies. 'So sorry Mr Jones,' she twittered meekly. 'It's my fault; I was late with breakfast this morning.'

'Not to worry Mrs Sykes,' said an uncomfortable Sid. He felt that at any moment the mousy Mrs Sykes might burst into tears, he certainly wasn't up to dealing with that.

At precisely 8 45am Major Sykes strutted out through his front door shouting over his shoulder, 'Two coffees out here Prue, toot sweet. Right then Jones, let's get started.' No word of apology from the blustering Major for his lateness.

Sid already had his ladder leaning up at the side of the cottage and began his ascent. He was no more than four rungs up when the Major called him back down. 'Coffee, Jones, come on man, chop chop.' Sid came back down his ladder feeling more than a little irritated. All he wanted to do was get on with the job. Finally, coffee downed, Sid began again to climb his ladder.

It didn't take Sid long to decide that there was a lot more years in this thatch before it would need attention. He came down his ladder and sought out the very bumptious Major Barnaby Sykes. Sid found him instructing his wife in the art of rose pruning. 'C'mon woman, get a move on, they should be pruned by 17th March. They won't be done by St Patrick's Day next year at this rate.'

Sid noticed that Barney had failed to tell his wife to cut just a 1/4 inch above a bud, and to be sure the cut angled away from the bud. Failure to do so could quite easily result in rainwater saturating and rotting it. *Their worry*, thought Sid to himself.

'Ah Jones, what news?' Asked Barney.

'All good Major Sykes, that thatch will probably see us both out.' Sid chuckled.

The Major looked at Sid and yelled, 'Call yourself a thatcher! Good God man, a fool can see it needs attention.' Sid was very taken aback at the vitriolic tirade aimed at him. His initial reaction was to bid the Major good day and take his leave, but Sid felt the need to explain his findings and tell the Major how he knew the thatched roof was not in a state of disrepair (if the man would listen). Luckily, or maybe, more unusually, the Major listened to what Sid had to say.

Sid described how the dry vegetation, Straw, Water Reed or Sedge, was layered in such a way that any water fell away from the inner roof and couldn't possibly leak. 'There's no wire netting covering the thatch,' stated Barney smugly. 'Everyone knows thatched roofs have to have that.'

'Well no, actually they don't. It has been proven over time that the wire covering reduces the longevity of the roof.' Sid knew his job and was able to stand his ground admirably against Barney. Sid went on to say 'As thatches are fixed or replaced these days, the wire netting is not replaced. Also the gads, the twisted hazel staples that hold the thatch in place, are not on view. If I could see the gads, I would certainly have concerns about your roof.'

Sid was enjoying his 'one-upmanship' and carried on. 'There is one other thing Major, the thickness of the thatch will decrease over a period of time. Hence the chance of seeing the gads. This is because the surface of the thatch will turn to compost over time. Certain weather conditions, wind and rain, will naturally remove the compost and the thatch becomes thinner. But this takes years, and a good thatch can last up to fifty years. Your roof was only replaced five years ago; I did it myself.'

'But the leak,' blustered the Major.

'Is not coming from the roof.' Said Sid.

Looking like Barney was going to fly off the handle, Sid thought he would leave before it happened. He fetched his ladder and placed it back inside his van. Said goodbye very quickly, and left.

Over the years things never improved between the two men, whenever one, or the other, could get a little dig in, they would. For Sid Jones, his moment of glory came when, quite by chance, he found out that the retired 'Major' was, in fact, an ex Salvation Army Major. He had never been attached to the military. Sid dined out on that little gem for a very long time, much to the annoyance of Barney Sykes.

Now, glaring at each other yet again, they were once more at loggerheads. Their fellow committee members had long since given up trying to get them to make peace. It was never going to happen, and while Sid was a very easy going man as a rule, and usually got on well with all of the villagers, Barney had upset everyone at some point.

Today's contretemps was about who did what in the church Spring Fayre. It was clear to see that nothing would be decided in this evenings meeting and it was hastily closed by the chairman. Both Sid and Barney left the meeting still arguing about the forthcoming event.

Sid was woken early next morning by a loud banging on his front door. Reaching for his dressing gown which was hanging from a hook on the back of the bedroom door, he smiled to himself.. 'Best not answer the door in the buff.' He padded barefoot down the steep, rickety stairs, putting his dressing gown on as he went. As he reached for the latch to open the door, there came another knock. Sid opened the door and was greeted by the village policeman.

'Morning Sid,' he said. 'Sorry to get you up so early, but I'm looking for a bit of information.'

'Morning Mick, I will help you if I can.' Said Sid, 'What do you want to know?' P.C. Mick Rawlings looked a little uncomfortable. 'Were you at the church committee meeting last night?'

'Yes' laughed Sid. 'Have you ever known me to miss a meeting, always looking for a chance to wind up Barney Sykes, those meetings are perfect.'

P.C. Rawlings didn't smile. 'Did you leave the church hall at the same time as Major Sykes?'

'He's not a Major you know,' interrupted Sid, 'That's just

what he wants folk to think, that he's better than the rest of us, and yes, I did.' At that moment the postman walked up the garden path and handed Sid his mail.

'I see the pompous old beggar finally got his just desserts.'

'Er, I haven't told him yet Sir,' said Constable Rawlings.

'Haven't told me what? What's going on?' Sid seemed very puzzled.

'Well,' said the postman; and was about to continue his story before being swiftly interrupted.

'Thank you, Sir,' Constable Rawlings said. He seemed keen to take over the conversation. The postman, looking disgruntled at having missed out on telling the best bit of gossip the village will have seen in years, walked away, happy in the knowledge that he had several more calls to make, and there would be ears eager to listen to what he had to say.

'What haven't you told me, Mick?' Sid asked the Constable.

'The Major is dead Sid; he was found this morning by his wife.' P.C. Rawlings looked suitably grave as he spoke the words.. 'Nasty business Sid.' Sid appeared lost for words for a few moments.

'So, what happened? A heart attack was it?' Hardly surprising really, always ranting about something. Surprised it didn't happen sooner. Still, a bit of a shock for Prudence, how's she coping? A bit of a nervy sort is old Prue.'

Constable Rawlings shook his head. 'Not too sure yet what has happened Sid, just making a few enquiries. May need to talk to you again.' Constable Rawlings said goodbye to Sid and walked down the garden path and through the little black wrought iron garden gate into the street.

Sid closed his front door and went into the kitchen, almost in a daze. He hadn't liked the bombastic Barney Sykes, but had he ever wished him dead? The rust coloured floor tiles in the kitchen were cold beneath Sid's bare feet, and he shuddered.

Several days passed and the village of Amphlett was a hive of police activity. Never before had the sleepy village seen so much action. Villagers were gathered in small groups around the village discussing the more delicate details of the death of 'Major' Barnaby Sykes. 'It was murder,' said one, 'Robbery gone wrong' said another.'Might be suicide,' another dared to suggest. Finally, a meeting in the Village Hall was arranged, for the police to make an announcement.

The hall was full to capacity, everyone eager to hear what the police had to say. By now, of course, everyone knew it was murder. However, how, why, who, and even where in the house, no one knew. Were they about to be told?

The Vicar, Reverend Huw Davies, stood up in front of a crowd that far surpassed his Sunday congregation. 'Ladies and Gentleman,' he shouted across the hall. 'Could I please have your attention, just for a moment.' The villagers stopped talking amongst themselves, and the hall fell silent. All eyes were upon the vicar. 'As you are all aware,' he began, 'We are in the midst of a horrid business. Our lovely village has been tainted by the untimely demise of 'Major' Barnaby Sykes.' There were a few mumbles in the room at this. 'I will hand over to Detective Inspector Craddock to explain the purpose of this meeting.'

D.I. Craddock was a rather heavy set man. His thick, dark, hair, flecked with grey, suggested he may be in his forties, his weathered face with its ruddy complexion said older. He cleared his throat.'I would like to thank you all for taking the time to come and listen to what I have to say. I won't keep you any longer than necessary.' He continued, 'My team and I are working very hard to get to the bottom of this crime, and I do believe we are very close to solving it. My colleagues and I do appreciate your cooperation, and hope that we can continue to rely upon your understanding.'

It was the fervent belief of several of the locals that Sid Jones would eventually be arrested for the murder of Barney Sykes, after all, hadn't they been sworn enemies since the day they met. Even someone as mild-mannered as Sid must have his breaking point, and, he had been questioned several times by the police. Oh yes, just a matter of time.

When the news broke that the murderer had finally been arrested, the villagers, on hearing the name of the perpetrator, were unbelieving. It was Mrs Prudence Sykes. The villagers had all been very supportive of the 'grieving widow' in her hour of need. 'That can't be right. It must be a mistake. No, I don't believe that', were just a few of the comments. Gradually, the full story emerged in the national newspapers, and the villagers, and of course, the rest of the country, were able to read the whole, sorry tale.

Before moving into Holly Cottage in the quiet village of Amphlett, Major and Mrs Sykes had been members of their local Salvation Army Church. Barney was a drummer in the Army band, and Prudence played the tambourine. All was well until church members found out that Major Sykes was stalking a young female band member. There was a choice given. Leave the church and go, or face up to your misdeeds when the police are informed. The former option was agreed upon, and the Sykes left quietly. Prudence Sykes forgave her husband's misdemeanour, though he chose to refer to it as his 'moment of madness.' He, however, seemed to hold his long-suffering wife responsible for everything that had gone wrong in his life. He bullied and belittled his wife at every given opportunity.

His downfall came the night he chose to play a drum solo on the wooden arm of his bedroom chair. Sid Jones had upset Barney in the church meeting, and he was angry. When Barney was mad, he took his temper out on the meek-mannered Prudence. That evening she went to bed to escape his verbal abuse, but he followed her into the bedroom. Barney sat in the bedroom armchair and took a metal meat skewer from his jacket. This was going to be his drumstick for this evenings drum recital. It was just another way to torment Prudence; he would keep her awake night after night with his drumming. The constant tip tapping sound of metal on wood. On this particular night, Prudence reacted a little differently. Before Barney realised what was happening, Prudence leapt from her bed and snatched the meat skewer from his hand. She immediately jabbed it into Barney's neck. She would stop his drumming once and for all. She continued stabbing the skewer in and out of her husband's neck several times.

Once she stopped her stabbing frenzy, she dropped the skewer and got back into bed where she lay quietly, listening to the gurgling sounds of her dying husband. She fell asleep to those sounds with a slight smile on her face.

Next morning Prudence got up. With barely a glance at her dead husband, she removed her bloodied nightdress and the bloodstained bedding and remade the bed. She then picked up the murder weapon. She showered and dressed, then, making sure the bed in the spare bedroom looked as though it had been slept in, she went downstairs and burned her bloodstained nightdress and the bed linen in the wood burning stove. She washed the metal skewer and placed it in the cutlery drawer.

After breakfast, she went upstairs and 'found' her husbands body. She phoned the police to report a crime. Someone had murdered her husband. Prudence Marjory Sykes was sat in the dock flanked by two women police officers. With her arms hanging limply at her sides, her shoulders hunched, and her head bowed, she was nervously awaiting sentence. Whilst initially she had tried to hide the fact that it was she who had murdered her husband, Major Barnaby Sykes, deep down, she knew she wouldn't get away with it.

Prudence wondered where it had all gone so horribly wrong,

how, and, more importantly, why? They had been happy once. Prudence and Barnaby met in the library, and, quite by chance. Prudence Wilson worked as a voluntary librarian once a week in her small, local library. She always worked on a Thursday. However, on this particular occasion, she had agreed to do Monday morning to cover for her colleague who had a medical appointment.

'Excuse me, Miss,' said a very stilted voice. Prudence looked up into the blue eyes of a man in his mid-thirties. 'I have had a letter from this establishment telling me my library books are overdue.' Prudence got very flustered, and dropped the book she was holding, as it fell, a loose page fluttered out of the book and floated down to the floor. Both adults had tried to catch the loose page as it floated past them. Leaning forwards, they missed the page, but their heads collided. 'Ouch,' they both said in unison. Then laughed. The blue-eyed man bent down and retrieved the book and loose page from the floor. He glanced at the page and stated, 'It's page thirty-seven, a bit of sticky tape will sort it.' Prudence felt herself going very pink when she realised that the man had not taken his eyes off her.

'You said something about a letter Mr... erm,' said a still flustered Prudence, as she took both book, and page, from his hand. He smiled and held out his hand to her. 'Barnaby Sykes, and you are?'

'Prudence... Prue Wilson,' she answered shyly. The thirty-year-old Prudence hadn't had much to do with the opposite sex. She was the only child of Agnes and Gilbert Wilson, a couple who met late in life, married, and got the shock of their lives when Agnes found herself expecting at the age of forty-three. Gilbert was fifty-one. As the offspring of older parents, Prudence had a very different upbringing to that of her peers. Agnes and Gilbert were overly protective and allowed her no freedom. She was sent to an all-girls school. No chance encounters with boys;

they wouldn't risk that. She couldn't follow fashion or listen to popular music.

As the years passed her parents, Agnes and Gilbert, relied more and more upon Prudence for her help. Life was passing her by. By the time she reached the age of thirty, she had no career, no friends and no social life. Both her parents finally succumbed to illness. Her mother when Prudence was twenty-three and her father, four years later, when she was twenty-seven. Fortunately, they left Prudence financially secure. The only good thing they did do for her.

All alone in the world, Prudence turned to charity work. She filled her empty life with hospital visits, charity shop work and of course, the local library. These activities did, at least, bring her into contact with other people. She gradually made a few friends and life started to be very enjoyable. She was, however, still painfully shy around men of a similar age to herself.

Barnaby Sykes reached into the inside pocket of his navy blue blazer and pulled out a letter. 'This was delivered to me on Saturday morning Miss Wilson,' stated Barnaby as he handed Prudence the letter. 'If you care to check your records, you will find that, not only have I returned the library books, but I returned them earlier than I needed to.

Prudence perused the letter for a few moments, then reached for a small wooden box marked with the letters S to V. Library book date cards were filed neatly within the small box. Very deftly, she flicked through the cards with her fingers, finally stopping when she found what she wanted. Prudence pulled a card from the box and studied it. 'Oh Mr Sykes, I can only apologise. There does indeed seem to have been a mistake. I can see you have returned the books, and yes, earlier than necessary.'

'No matter now Miss Wilson,' said a very amiable Barnaby Sykes. 'I am sure it won't happen again. Maybe we will meet again; I am often in the library. Goodbye.'

Prudence was just about to say to him she only worked Thursdays as a rule, but he had already moved away from the desk and was heading out of the door.

Prudence was only working till lunchtime and had popped to the staff room to get her coat and bag. When she came back through to the library, a colleague met her at the door. 'Ere Prue, there's a chap asking after you. Ee's right posh.'

'Really,' said a surprised Prudence. 'I wonder who that can be. Did he say what he wanted?'

'Nah, ee just asked to 'ave a word.' Her colleague seemed slightly bored.

When Prudence came through the door into the library, she was surprised to see Barnaby Sykes standing by the librarian's desk holding a bunch of gorgeous, cream roses. 'Mr Sykes,' said Prudence.

'Ah, Miss Wilson, I am so glad I caught you. I would like you to accept these if you would. It's just a small thank you for sorting things earlier for me.' Prudence had never been given flowers before, and indeed, never by a man. Feeling her cheeks growing pinker by the second, and getting very flustered, Prudence thanked Barnaby very much and tried to explain that she had only ascertained that a mistake had been made and that he should not have received the letter.

Barnaby smiled, 'Miss Wilson, will you please do me the honour of having lunch with me? That's if you don't have other plans of course.' Prudence blushed some more, and replied, 'That would be very nice Mr Sykes, thank you.'

'Please,' said Barnaby, 'Stop calling me Mr Sykes. Barnaby or Barney will be fine, and maybe you will allow me to call you Prue?' Prudence smiled her approval.

After a whirlwind romance, they married. It was a very quiet wedding with just a few guests. A meal in a local restaurant ended the day. There was no honeymoon. Time passed, and things seemed okay for a while.

As a Salvation Army Major, Barnaby had welcomed Prudence into the Citadel, and their lives were spent doing charitable work and playing in the band. However, it soon became very apparent to Prudence that Barnaby was a stern man. He liked his way, and he wanted things done in a precise manner. When things were put in cupboards, they were placed in a particular order. Hand towels in the bathroom had to be folded in a certain way. Shirts were ironed and folded as though just out of the box. Barnaby liked his socks rolled into a ball and placed in his drawer in rows of matching colours. If any of these things were incorrect, Barnaby would chastise Prudence as you might a child, and he would tell her she was stupid and useless. Eventually, she believed him.

Barnaby Sykes had one weakness. Young women. He thought himself to be dashing and handsome. In his former years, he possibly was. Reaching his fifties, he wasn't the catch he thought he was. He would proposition young women wherever, and whenever, he pleased. He paid no heed to the fact that he was married. Prudence counted for nothing. She was just the mousy woman he married, and, more importantly, she kept the house as he wanted it to be preserved. She also did as she was told.

Eventually, as Barnaby made more of a fool of himself, and annoyed more and more people, Prudence turned a blind eye to his misdemeanours and learned to ignore the pitying glances and the whisperings as she went about her business. When the Salvation Army finally realised what their esteemed 'Major' was up to, and the ultimatum voiced, it was almost a relief to Prudence to move away and start afresh where no one knew them, or, more importantly, didn't know about Barnaby's 'peccadillo.'

This was a new beginning. Sadly, it wasn't quite that

straightforward. The village of Amphlett was beautiful, and the people friendly. However, yet again, Barnaby began to annoy people almost as soon as they had moved in. The residents of Amphlett were mainly of retirement age or nearing it. Not many younger women to be propositioned by the ageing lothario, so he turned his attentions instead, to arguing with anyone and everyone.

He made himself extremely unpopular, and had turned the unassuming, and very timid Prudence into a near recluse. She visited the village store only when necessary, choosing instead to telephone her main shopping requirements to shops in the nearby town. These items were delivered to Holly Cottage on a regular basis.

The couple attended church every Sunday, and whilst Barnaby served on the Church Committee, Prudence chose to give her services in a way that prevented her having to spend too much time in the village. She didn't want to inflict her stupidity on the villagers, so she baked cakes for the cake sales that were held regularly for varying charities. She could always find items for the tombola stall that was popular at the annual summer fete. Christmas would find her making pretty table decorations to be sold at the winter bazaar.

To think it would end like this, no one could have imagined. 'ALL RISE.' Prudence stood up and glanced around the courtroom. She could see the jury. Her fate was in the hands of these twelve strangers. Looking up at the very full gallery, Prudence recognised all of the faces. Villagers had turned up to support her, but she found herself searching for one face in particular. The face of Sid Jones. Sid had been a tower of strength since the incident. He had supported Prudence from the very moment he had heard just how she had been treated by that rotten husband of hers. He smiled down at her. She shyly smiled back, relieved that he was here and still supporting her.

The Judge was about to address the jury, he had been speaking, but Prudence wasn't focussing on him. She was looking at Sid for strength. 'On the charge of murder, how do you find the defendant, Prudence Marjory Sykes? Guilty or Not Guilty?' The Judge spoke clearly and precisely.

The Foreman of the Jury replied... ' Not Guilty.'

'On the charge of manslaughter, how do you find the defendant, Prudence Marjory Sykes? Guilty or Not Guilty?' Again the words were clear and precise.

The Foreman of the Jury replied... 'Guilty.'

'Is this the verdict of you all?' Enquired the Judge.

'Yes M'lord,' replied the foreman.

There was a hushed silence in the courtroom. Everyone knew that sentencing was next. Sid leaned forward in his seat, he looked at Prudence, she glanced up at him, and he nodded his head as if to say, 'don't worry Prue, you'll be okay.'

She nodded back, then stood firmly, awaiting her fate. The Judge began to speak. 'Prudence Marjory Sykes, you have been found guilty of manslaughter, and I have now to pass sentence.' He continued, 'It is my firm belief that you were driven to this desperate act of violence due to the cruel and thoughtless actions of your victim. Years of mental abuse from your late husband pushed you to the very limit. I do not believe you are a danger to anyone else; therefore I am sentencing you to three years, of which two and a half will be suspended. You have already served six months on remand. You are free to go Mrs Sykes.'

He smiled. 'Go and enjoy the remainder of your life.' Prudence stepped out of the dock in a daze and was bustled away by the two policewomen. She was taken from the court to a waiting car. Sat in the driver's seat was Sid. He beamed at her and said, 'Come on Prue, let's get you home.'

'But where is home now Sid?' Prue asked. 'I can't go back to

Holly Cottage. I couldn't live there again.'

'I am taking you home with me, he answered. 'You need looking after; it's about time someone cared for you.'

Prue leaned across and kissed Sid's cheek. 'Thank you, Sid.'

He chuckled and said, 'I think you and I will rub along very nicely together.'

I, the narrator of the story, thinks they will too.

The Restaurant

Not too many tables free at present. The young couple cast their eyes around the room, which one would be best?. Suddenly they move forward and make a dash for a table for two in the corner. She is sure that another couple have their eye on it. With a few twists and turns, a couple of bobs, and even a twirl, the couple reach their chosen table and lay claim to it with a carefully placed jacket on the back of the chair. They then make their way back to the counter to study the specials board.

'What d'ya fancy? He asked. She had her arm around him, and her hand on his bum, I am presuming they are boyfriend and girlfriend. 'Dunno love, sommat with chips I think.' Was his answer, with not much enthusiasm. 'What you 'aving?'

His girlfriend raised her eyebrows. 'You live on chips you do, why don't you 'ave sommat healthy? I might 'ave a salad,' she said, looking very virtuous. Then she said 'Can I pinch a few of your chips?' He turned and looked at his girlfriend. Shaking his head, he laughed. 'Oh very healthy I'm sure. Don't the calories count if they are my chips then?' She laughed back at him and said. 'Oh you, shall we both 'ave sommat and chips?' They both decided on Lasagne, and it came with chips, salad, and garlic bread.

After ordering, they made their way back to their table, carrying two coffees and their cutlery, serviettes and an assortment of condiments in small plastic sachets. Sitting on the table next to them are an elderly couple. They have a pot of tea for two. They also have cake. She has a nice simple slice of Madeira, and he has gone for the gooey chocolate cake. 'Shall we go halves?' Asked the elderly lady, somewhat hopefully. He looked at her, it was a look that said, 'Did you just suggest I share my chocolate cake?' He looked away, almost as though he hadn't heard her, or maybe wished he hadn't, but she wasn't giving in easily. 'I said shall we go halves with our cake?' Poor man, he obviously didn't want to share his cake, but begrudgingly said, 'Yes, if you want to.' The two cakes were duly cut in half, and, as she passed him his half slice of Madeira, and reached for half of his chocolate cake, his facial expression suggested that this was far from a fair swap, in his mind anyway.

The queue at the counter isn't getting any smaller. The poor staff are rushed off their feet. 'Have you got any more knives? Ooh, there isn't any vinegar. Ask if they have more sugar.' The requests were coming thick and fast. The one young girl was bobbing up and down behind the counter like a small boat on the ocean, trying to find the required items from the shelving underneath.

On the big table in the centre of the restaurant, there seems to be a celebration taking place. There is a lot of reference to The Birthday Girl. The 'girl' in question is very easily well over the first flush of youth, and probably several more flushes besides. No matter, she is thoroughly enjoying being the centre of attention. Gaily coloured gift bags and pretty parcels bedecked with bows are being passed around the table until they reach the eager recipient. 'Ooh, this is wonderful,' she proclaimed. I wondered where they might place their food when it was brought to the table. Drinks and gifts were taking up most of the space available.

The birthday girl clapped her hands with glee as she opened a small brightly wrapped gift. 'My favourite talc, I adore the smell of lavender.' The 'party' guests all smiled.

Back at the table for two, the young couple are busy passing their food from plate to plate. Having had it delivered to their table, she has decided she will never eat it all. 'Will you 'ave some of my chips, and my garlic bread?' 'Pass it over then,' said the obviously hungry young man.'I think I can manage the extra.' He gave her a big grin. Finally sorted, they start tucking in.

Looking around I see that the elderly couple have gone. Their table has been taken by an older gentleman and, I presume, his middle-aged daughter. 'I think I'll have the fish,' he said. 'What does it come with?'

'Don't know,' was her reply. 'Shall I go and ask?'

'No, I will have it how it comes, I'm not fussy,' He smiled, and watched, as she went to the counter to order. What the gent did next rather shocked me. He took from the inside pocket of his jacket, a pair of nail clippers and proceeded to cut his fingernails. His dining companion came back to the table and sat down. She said nothing to him about his activity, apparently unconcerned. Maybe she was used to it, and that's why she wasn't bothered. It bothered me.

I was right, the waitress has brought the food to the birthday girls table, and there is very little space to place it down. Parcels and bags are being lifted or swept to one side in a frantic attempt to make room for the meals. 'Ooh, careful with that one,' someone shrieked. 'It's breakable.' Finally, calm ensued, and they settled down. Calm lasted for a short while only, then up went the shout, 'Happy Birthday Marjory.' An array of teacups, coffee mugs, and water glasses were held aloft in a toast to the birthday girl. She came over all silly and giggled her thank you. Happily, they refrained from breaking into a rousing rendition of Happy Birthday, opting instead, to save that for the evening barbeque, which they had been discussing at great length. Silence followed as the food was eaten.

A sullen child scrapes the topping off her pizza, she tells her mother its horrible and nothing like the one she has at home. Mummy is busy with the baby brother who seems intent on making as much mess as possible on the highchair tray. Maybe leaving the cake on the plate would have been a better option.

Who knows. The sullen child continues playing with her pizza. 'Oh for goodness sake Millie,' said her irate mother. 'Pizza is pizza. Stop messing with it, just eat your chips and peas.'

On the next table to myself, two women have just settled themselves down. They haven't visited the counter, so I think they are hoping for waitress service. It's early afternoon, and it looks as though they are here for afternoon tea. Maybe it was pre-booked. The waitress has just brought two beautiful china cups and saucers to their table, but they don't match. How odd... No pun intended. One cup and saucer is pink, the other blue. Next comes a charming china teapot. Again, it doesn't match either of the cups and saucers. This is starting to look decidedly less high-end afternoon tea and more, let's give it a go and see what happens.

Everything is being brought to the table in dribs and drabs. Next to arrive is a stone coloured hot water jug, and milk jug and sugar bowl. The milk jug and sugar bowl match the teapot, well that's something. I can't help wondering why they didn't just use a tray and carry everything in one go. The final arrival, of course, is the star of the show. The three-tiered cake stand, complete with cakes. The waitress placed the stand on the table, and I think all eyes were upon it as it started to lean to one side. Breath was held as we all waited for the cake selection to slowly slide off the stand. Thankfully it didn't happen, but the cake stand listed precariously, and its sweet treats looked somewhat like an edible leaning tower of Pisa. Thinking that the Tea For Two could now begin in earnest, out came the waitress yet again. Two small pots were set down on the table. The contents, jam and cream for the scones. One of the ladies then left the table and went to the counter. She came back to the table carrying two plain tea plates and two teaspoons. Apparently, the waitress had forgotten to bring these items on one of the many trips to and from the table.

Now, a little more mismatched crockery, not even pretty china plates, and worse still, no pastry forks. A nice piece of coffee and walnut cake, a delicious slice of Victoria sandwich or lemon drizzle cake warrants a dainty pastry fork. Never a teaspoon. Surprisingly, there didn't appear to be a savoury option, but maybe that was their choice. It all looked lovely though, and the two ladies in question barely exchanged a word as they tucked into their cakes and pastries. But the presentation and the numerous trips to and from the kitchen all seemed a bit casual. For me anyway, afternoon tea should be a special treat. I felt the two ladies deserved better. In my mind, they had been cheated of the very delightful experience it could have and should have, been. There wasn't even a tablecloth.

I notice that young Millie finally cleared her plate. Pizza obviously wasn't so bad after all. She is giving her mum five minutes to eat her sandwich and drink her cuppa by playing peek a boo with her brother. They are both laughing loudly. Not such a sullen child after all. It has been an interesting lunchtime. As a food writer and critic, I eat in many establishments and see people from all walks of life. I have eaten food, good, and bad, in equal measure. Great food can be found in a local pub, sometimes, even better food can be found at a roadside caravan. Fancy restaurants and high prices do not always produce good food. My fayre today was a simple panini with bacon and brie and a side order of chips. Homemade chips. Not the frozen, cardboard type, oven chip favoured by so many eateries today.

My report will reflect on my own food only, and it will be a good, honest report. I could not possibly comment on the afternoon tea, but you can be sure I will be back to sample one. Then, and only then, will I be able to say what my opinion is. Time to go, people are waiting for my table.

Hope

Aunt Stella beckoned me to follow her. She's not as agile as she used to be, but is still moving at a fair old pace. She's getting on in years, but remains relatively healthy, all things considered.

Aunt Stella is my dad's sister. I haven't seen him in years, well, he never did take his parenting duties very seriously. Oh, don't get me wrong, he came sniffing around my mother a few times over the years, but eventually, the visits stopped. No great loss there. He liked the ladies.

Mum brought me up with help from Aunt Stella. Mum was knocked down and killed last year. She didn't stand much chance against the lorry, which was travelling at speed. Aunt Stella told me it was quick and she didn't suffer. I take great comfort from that. Heaven knows where we are going.

I feel as though we have walked miles. 'Come on Fuzz Bum, hurry up.' Aunt Stella always calls me Fuzz Bum, I have no clue as to why, and neither does she. My name is actually Hope.

We had been walking, or rather, racing, down the High Street, but she has turned off down an alley I didn't even know existed. The streets are quiet. It's nearly dusk, and curfew will start soon. We shouldn't even be out. I am very nervous, and it is unusual for my Aunt to be so cavalier about rules. 'FUZZ BUM, WILL YOU PLEASE HURRY.' I followed her down the alley, which was only a few yards long. At the end of the alley was a door, a brightly painted door. With dusk fast approaching, the alley was getting dark, but even in this half-light, the door glowed almost magically. It was canary yellow in colour and, well... it glowed. There didn't appear to be a door handle, a door knocker, or even a letterbox.

Aunt Stella told me to look, and learn. I looked. Aunt Stella leaned very gently to the right, onto the wall of the alley.

Immediately the door quietly opened. If I live forever, I will never forget the sight that my eyes feasted upon. I can only say that wherever I looked were books, books, and even more books. At first glance, it looked as though the books were open to the elements and very much in danger of being damaged. On closer inspection, a perspex roof seemed to envelop the whole alley. I looked around in sheer amazement.

My Aunt told me to hurry inside so the door could be closed. It was very surreal, this feeling of being in a library, yet knowing it was still just an alley.

There was an open door at the end of the book filled area, and more books were clearly visible. 'It's all yours Fuzz Bum.' My Aunt broke into my reverie. 'Every book that sits here in this place belongs to you, for now. 'Your mother willed them to you, and you have to promise to keep them safe until the world is ready to receive them again. These books belong to all people, you are only the guardian, and have ownership for as long as it takes.'

I was confused and asked what she meant by 'for as long as it takes.' I could never have been prepared for her answer. 'We haven't always been answerable to cats Fuzz Bum, we were humans in charge of our own destiny once. Then the cats came. They had no use of books and learning. 'We all knew that cats were fast taking over certain places around the globe. Measures were taken to protect important tomes, and people held in high esteem were chosen as guardians of these works. There are alleys like this one in cities across the world, and they are in secret locations and guarded closely by the chosen few.'

I had a million questions, but Aunt Stella was way ahead of me. She began to tell me that fifteen years ago (a year before I was born) a small island in Africa had been taken over by Cats. The inhabitants of the small island were helpless against the cats. They begged for help from bigger nations, but the support didn't come, and within a month of the takeover there were no books to be found on the island. The cats had destroyed them all.

Word got out that the cats were controlling more and more of the world and destroying everything that could be deemed to pass on knowledge. That is when the secret libraries were thought up. Surely, there would come a time when humans would take back their planet?

Cats are controlling creatures, they have no need of humans. They can fend for themselves. They knew that humans needed rules and regulations, they needed companionship, they needed human contact. They also knew they had a thirst for knowledge. The cats believed that in taking away the items that provided the knowledge humans craved, they could finally rule the world. They were right. With no places of learning and no way of providing an education, young people quickly lost their way. With tutors and teachers out of work boredom set in, arguments broke out, and the cats were gradually taking away the freedom of the human.

My Aunt carried on her story. 'It didn't take very long for the world to succumb to cat control. They began to make rules for humans to live by, and like the weak fools, we are we followed these rules. Cats keep producing kittens and in only a few months per cycle more and more cats rule. Our only strength is here and places like here. Wherever there are books, we have places of learning. We have to spread the word quietly and efficiently to any who will risk coming here to learn. One day we will be ready to rebel. When that day comes, we need people who have the knowledge to pass on to others. That knowledge starts here. Your mother believed that you can lead the way. That's why she called you Hope. You ARE Hope.'

The Diary

The young woman pulled her woollen shawl tightly around her shoulders. It was chilly on deck tonight. She shivered, but as she did so, strong arms wrapped around her. 'Here you are Millie, I wondered where you had got to.' Millie Roberts leaned back into the warm body of her new husband, Charles. 'It's such a beautiful night Charles,' whispered Millie, 'look at the sky. Have you ever seen so many stars?' '

Why would I look at the stars? I would rather look at you.'Charles said.

Millie laughed. 'You always say the right thing, Charles. Promise me you always will.'

Charles turned her towards him and smiled. 'Always my darling, always. Come on, let's walk, we'll be warmer.'

The young couple huddled together as they walked. Millie and Charles had married a few days previously in the small French town of Chef-du-Pont, just twenty-three miles from Cherbourg. Millie's mother was French, and Millie was adamant she would not marry if her beloved Grand-mere Dubois was not present at her wedding. Madame Dubois was considered too feeble to travel to England for her granddaughter's wedding, so the wedding party travelled to her.

As they strolled the deck under the star emblazoned sky, Millie and Charles recalled the happy day. The walk on cobblestones, through the narrow streets of Chef-du-Pont to the little church, which had been decorated with spring flowers. The wedding service, conducted in French and English, and the wedding breakfast. A magnificent feast of cold meats, French cheeses and rich, creamy desserts. Then there were the fine wines with which to wash it all down. Yes, they agreed. The day had been excellent, the happiest of days.

They would have to wait for the photographs, but no matter, they would be worth waiting for. However, they couldn't help wondering what they would be like. Had the photographer managed to catch the antics of the two small bridesmaids? So prettily dressed in their elegant pink gowns, miniature replicas of the brides own white bridal gown. Their blonde curls bedecked with little pink rosebuds. Had he captured the impish behaviour of the sailor-suited pageboy? How they both hoped that he had.

It was a little after ten thirty, the night was growing colder. The newlyweds had danced the evening away in the chandeliered ballroom and were more than ready to return to their cabin. Saying goodnight to the other passengers braving the cold night air, they made their way back to their cabin, grateful for the warmth that it offered.

Charles settled himself in bed, but Millie was determined to write her diary first. She had made a vow to herself that she would keep a diary from day one of her marriage. One day she would show it to the daughter they both hoped for. Let her see what a happy life her parents had. How much they loved each other and hopefully, the kind of happy union, she could have when she met the right man.

Millie closed her diary, marking the following day's page with the white satin ribbon that she had worn woven through her hair on the day of her wedding. She slipped into bed beside her husband and, wrapped in each other's arms, they fell into a deep slumber. Neither of them felt the liner judder and stop. They were not aware that the engines had gone silent. Millie didn't see the white, leather-bound diary fall to the floor of the cabin, open at a page dated April 15th 1912. The newlyweds had boarded HMS Titanic in Cherbourg alongside nineteen others on April 10th. Two days after their wedding. Sixteen of those twenty-one passengers survived. Millie and Charles Roberts did not.

Mum

It's the weekend, and kids go to their dads from Saturday morning until Sunday teatime. BLISS.

Every Saturday starts the same, I lie in bed listening to the kids getting their overnight bags packed. I don't interfere, they know exactly what they want to take with them. Will they know where everything is? Probably not. I may as well get up, the yelling will start soon.

Kettle on, teabag in a favourite mug. The mug is white china, I think tea tastes so much better from a china vessel. Emblazoned across the side of the mug in big purple letters is just one word. MINE. Everyone knows it is, and they never use it.

'Mum, where's my Little Mix tee shirt?' My twelve-year-old daughter Amy shouts from the lounge.

'Certainly not in the lounge Amy,' is my speedy reply.

'Well, where then,' she yelled back. The beginning of yet another pre-teenage strop.

'Try your bedroom, Amy.' She stomps off upstairs.

'Have you seen my football boots, mum? I can't find them.' I'm listening to Ben, my fourteen-year-old son, scrabbling about in the shoebox that lives under the stairs.

'They are in the shoe box Ben, I put them there myself last night, look a bit harder,' I told him.

'They must be invisible then,' was his cocky reply, 'Because I can't find them.'

'I wish I was invisible Ben,' I responded. 'Maybe then, if you and your sister couldn't see me, you may start thinking, and doing, a little bit more for yourselves.' That, of course, was met with stony silence.

Eventually, all items required were traced and packed. It was eleven o'clock, there was a knock on the door. It was my ex, on time, as always. He is a stickler for punctuality. The kids rush off down the path towards their father's car. Not even a backwards glance at me, stood here, waving to them. I resist the temptation to run a lap of the lawn yelling freedom. I opt instead to close the front door and go upstairs and change from my tatty tracksuit into something a little smarter.

I choose a pale grey sweater and black and grey midi skirt. I put on my black, lace-up ankle boots and wrap a black, silk scarf around my neck. I am now ready to face the world.

Once downstairs, I grab my bag, check I have book, purse and house keys. All present and correct, I go out through the front door, slamming it shut behind me. It's a lovely day, I am going to walk to the park, find myself a park bench to sit on, and I'm going to read my book. En route I pop into the local corner shop and purchase a chicken sandwich, a bottle of water and a banana. I'm going to have a picnic in the park.

It is only a short walk from home to the park, as I enter the big, open black wrought iron gates, it feels like a different world. The traffic noise subsides, all I hear is the rustling of leaves on the trees as the breeze gently weaves through their branches, and the quacking and honking of ducks and geese being fed by excited youngsters. This is what weekends are made for.

I stroll around for a while until I find a wooden bench where I can sit and read my book, or, just watch the world go by. I settle myself down and take the book from my bag. I haven't been reading for very long, but suddenly I become aware that I am being stared at. I look up, there is a young couple stood in front of me, hand in hand. 'That's brilliant,' the young girl said, looking at her boyfriend. 'I wonder how it's done?' 'Dunno, it's clever though,' her boyfriend replied. I looked behind me, wondering what on earth they were looking at. The girl gave an excited squeal and did a kind of jig. 'OMG, she moves as well. Did you see that Danny, did you, did you?' Before he had time to answer his overexcited girlfriend, I asked them, 'Are you looking at me?'

'OMG, she talks as well Danny.' She did the silly jig again, and I was beginning to lose patience. Being some form of free entertainment was not how I intended spending my Saturday, especially as I had no idea how I was doing it.

'Could you please give me some clue as to what you find so interesting about me?' I asked, as politely as I could.

'You're invisible, it's amazing,' stated the excitable one. I may not be an exceptionally logical person, but even I know, that if I were invisible, they couldn't see me. As they can see me, I am clearly, not invisible. I pointed this out to the pair. 'We can only see your clothes,' they both shouted.'We can't see your head or your hands.' I looked down at my book, and they were right. My hands weren't there. My book was suspended in mid-air, or at least, that's what it looked like. How could that be? I could feel the book in my hands, I just couldn't see my hands. I let out a yell and dropped the book. 'What has happened to me?' I screamed.

The girl did the jig thing again, now thoroughly convinced that I was the weekend entertainment. I pull my scarf up over my head, grab my bag and hurriedly leave the park. My heart is beating like a drum, and I need to get home. The book I just forgot about and left it lying on the ground where I had dropped it.

I reach home in double quick time and almost fall into the house. I slam the front door shut, race up the stairs and into my bedroom. The wardrobe boasts a full-length mirror, in trepidation, I step in front of it. I close my eyes, what if I can't see me when I open them. What do I expect to see? Well, me of course. Only I can't. I'm not there. My clothes are, but my physical being isn't.

Slowly, I remove my clothes. As I do so, there is less to see, until finally, there is nothing left to see at all. No reflection whatsoever. My mind is working overtime. How could this happen? Why did this happen to me? When did it happen? Would I change back? Maybe I'm asleep, yes, that's it. I'm dreaming. I will wake up soon. That isn't going to happen though. I know I am awake already. This is no dream, it's a living nightmare.

Slumping down on my bed, I can feel the tears stinging my eyes. I'm scared. These things don't happen to people in real life. It's what happens in films and books... isn't it? What if I never have a visible body again I ask myself. How will I explain this to Amy and Ben, to their Father, to anyone? I

lie back on my pillows and close my eyes. There are so many things going around and around in my head. I have to find out what has happened to me and why.

I open my eyes, and it's dark. I must have fallen asleep. Glancing at the bedside clock, I see the time is nearly ten o'clock, must have been sleeping for hours. As I rise from the bed, I catch a glimpse of myself. My physical body has returned. I don't know whether to laugh or cry. The relief I am feeling is immense. My one single thought is, at least I won't have to try and explain to the kids my invisibility. Throwing my dressing gown on to cover my far from perfect, naked body, I decide I am hungry and head off downstairs to the kitchen to make myself something to eat. My relief lasts all of a few moments. As I place my foot on the bottom stair, I realise I have disappeared.

I sit in the kitchen, wondering what on earth I am going to do. Surely this isn't a medical matter? I cannot possibly go to my doctor and tell him I keep disappearing. In my head, I play out the scenario. 'Morning Doctor.'

'Morning Carol, and what brings you here today? We don't see you very often.'

'You will possibly not see me at all soon, especially if it happens when I'm still here.'

'If what still happens Carol?'

'If I turn invisible. It happens for no apparent reason, other than, it seems, I just can.'

Doctor phones men in white coats... In my head, the doctor isn't an option. Maybe I should just cut out the middleman and find myself a good psychiatrist. Am I having some kind of nervous breakdown? I really don't think that I am.

Perhaps, instead of the downside, I should look for the positives in my situation. There surely has to be some. Being a naturally interested person (interested sounds so much more helpful than nosy) I could listen to many a conversation without anyone knowing. It would be handy if, once in a while, I went with the kids to their dads. They come back home with an attitude, I'm always wondering if he gives in to them, or talks about me in a less than positive way. But, the negatives creep in. If I suddenly become visible how on earth do I explain my presence? There is only one thing for it. I must speak to someone, and very soon. But who?

Even as I sit here, I have become aware that my physical form has reappeared. Is this my life from here on in? Now you see me, oops, now you don't. Am I destined to spend my life in the shadows? Only going out after dark like some modern day vampire. Or perhaps I will never go out again. Do I, starting from now, begin living my life like a hermit, and never leave the house. That cannot be an option.

Could I google invisibility I wonder, but it will only tell me what I already know? If something is invisible, it cannot be seen. When I think of the times, I wished there was less of me, but I did mean less, not nothing at all, which is the case right now.

My form has gone again. Nestling amongst the untidy pile of different books that are precariously balanced on the corner of the kitchen table, I spot an old Yellow Pages telephone directory. Will I find a solution to my predicament in there? It's certainly worth a look, what have I got to lose?

The sun is coming up. I have been here all night, reading this directory like a novel. One page at a time. On the table are an empty wine bottle, my china mug and a half-eaten packet of crisps. Salt and Vinegar flavour, not my favourite, and, they were out of date.

On and off all night, my visibility and invisibility have come and gone with some regularity. It seems to change hourly. Interestingly, when I eat or drink in my invisible state, I could not see the food and drink travelling through my body. Thank goodness for small mercies. How off-putting would that have been?

I have a phone number. Life Coach. Not too sure whether there will be anything helpful to be gained, but I have to start somewhere. As soon as nine o'clock comes, I will phone. Hopefully, someone will answer, I am very aware it is Sunday. First and foremost though, I need to dress, even though I could spend twelve hours a day, not being seen, standards cannot slip, and I daresay the winter will still be felt whether I can be seen or not. Though, please God, let this debacle be over long before winter arrives.

I'm wondering whether to shower. I would normally, but, this isn't normal. My decision is made. Not bothering today, I'm not planning on going anywhere, it won't hurt for one day. The clock seems to be going backwards, hurry up nine o'clock, the need to share my dilemma is becoming all-consuming. I have to tell someone else, and, as soon as I can. In my head, I am convinced that once I have spoken about this to someone else, everything will be sorted... won't it?

Pottering in the kitchen keeps me busy, I have washed my mug. Usually, tea would be my chosen beverage, but coffee will help me stay awake, even though I did sleep throughout the evening yesterday, I had no sleep overnight. The kettle boils just as the clock strikes nine. Coffee hurriedly made, I key the number into my phone, pick up my coffee and go into the lounge.

As I sit in my armchair, a man's voice in my ear says, 'Good morning, Ross Palmer speaking, how may I help you?' He has a voice as smooth as melted chocolate. My immediate thought is, he will either be a very gorgeous man or a slimeball. I take a deep breath, and out it all pours. After a few minutes of my incoherent ramblings, he interrupts me. 'Er, excuse me Miss, Mrs, erm Ms?' So intent in telling my tale of woe, I haven't even told him who I am.

'Sorry, my name is Carol. Mrs Carol James.

'Ok, is it alright for me to call you Carol?' That smooth voice had a very calming effect. We have been speaking for several minutes when Ross Palmer asks me if he can come to the house. I'm not usually a woman who encourages house visits, and certainly not by men I have never met. On this particular occasion, I allay my fears because I need help from someone, and at least he hasn't laughed at what I have told him. That is what I expected. I immediately agree to him visiting and give him my address. He tells me he will be straight here. It isn't even nine thirty. I do hope the neighbours aren't up and about early, they will wonder why the divorcee from number twenty-three is entertaining a man so early on a Sunday morning.

Wonder what he charges, it has just struck me that this wouldn't be a free service. It never entered my head to ask him, I was too busy telling him about the couple in the park, my sleepless night and of course my strange appearances and disappearances.

He's here, knocking at my door. At least I am here too, he will see me, for now anyway. I open the door and there he is, Ross Palmer. If ever a voice doesn't match the picture of the person you visualise in your head, then this is it. He is very tall and gangly, a bit geeky looking. About forty-something I imagine and not too fashion conscious. Can you still even buy corduroy trousers? His hair is greying, and a trim wouldn't go amiss, it is very straggly and catching on the collar of his beige flowery shirt. It seems as though he is stuck in a particular decade though I am not confident which one it may be.

He introduces himself, and I invite him in and show him into the lounge. Would he like tea or coffee? Apparently neither! There is an air of awkwardness between us, and I am beginning to think that maybe he does believe me to be mad, or perhaps he doesn't want to miss the golden opportunity of seeing a woman disappear before his very eyes. Finally, he speaks. 'Carol, you may be surprised to hear that you are not the first person this has happened to, you probably won't be the last. Are you prepared to listen to what I have to say?'

He goes on to say that he could help me and that timing was a huge part of the help I required. As I agree to listen, I disappear. Ross seems entirely unfazed by this.

'Carol, you may not be aware that for just one brief moment in time we all are granted one wish. Wishes are being granted every day. Sadly, these wishes are not all good. We are human, and we wish for things without thought.' He said.

I was looking at him and thinking, maybe he is the mad one. 'Have you ever wished you were invisible Carol. We wish for all sorts of things, don't we? The throwaway wish. I wish you would go away, I wish you'd drop dead, I wish I could win the lottery, I wish I could get a decent job. The list of wishes goes on and on. In the brief moment, it is your turn, time stands still for you, and your wish is granted. You won't even notice. I must ask you again Carol. Have you ever wished you were invisible?'

In a flash, I think back to yesterday, and the conversation about Bens football boots. 'I wish I was invisible Ben, then maybe?' 'Yes,' I murmur. 'I said it to my son yesterday morning.'

'Can you remember the time Carol? This is most important.'

'I'm not sure,' I tell him.

'Please try and think Carol, we have a very tight timeframe if this is to be reversed.'

'How tight?' I ask. His answer surprised me.

'About fifteen minutes, if we don't succeed in the time frame today, twenty-four hours after the wish was granted then you wait until next week and try again.

The kids were picked up at eleven, it had to be somewhere between ten and ten thirty. I glance at the clock, its ten minutes past ten. 'Right then, let's give it a go.' Ross jumped up and asked where the conversation had taken place. 'In the kitchen, I told him, at least, that's where I was. Ben was under the stairs looking in the shoebox.'

'OK, I want you to say what it was you said to your son yesterday morning. Can you be as close to where you were when you said it.'

Who is this man I'm wondering? 'Is this going to work?' I ask.

'Fortunately, you are still invisible so we should know fairly quickly. Now please, hurry. Say what you have to say.' He answered.

I feel a bit stupid, but needs must, here goes. 'I wish I was invisible Ben, maybe then, if you and your sister couldn't see me, you may start thinking, and doing, a little bit more for yourselves.' Looking at Ross, I smile, and say. 'Now what.'

He smiles back at me, and says, 'Welcome back Carol.' Holding my arms out in front of me I can see my hands again. Relief surges through my body. 'Am I back for good? I ask'

'Yes Carol, you are.' He answers.

I ask him how he knows about this strange thing that happens. He just smiled and started saying goodbye. What do I owe you? 'Nothing' was his reply. 'But surely you need payment? I ask. He doesn't answer, he just walks out of the front door and closes it behind him. I run to the lounge window, he's nowhere to be seen, how can that be? Maybe I will phone him later, offer some form of payment, perhaps a charity donation. I will get the number from the kitchen, I left the paper with his number written on it on the kitchen table.

It isn't here. Strange, it's where I left it. No matter, it's in Yellow Pages, but that seems to have disappeared too. I can see a piece of paper under the table, found it. I pick the paper up, it's the paper I wrote the number on, but the number isn't there. On the paper, just six words are written, in handwriting that is unfamiliar to me. 'Be Careful What You Wish For'.

The Silence

The silence in the lounge was almost deafening. George sat in his armchair gazing into space. He had sat in that same armchair for nearly twenty years, it was way past its best. The seat was sinking, and the arms were grubby. It was in quite a sorry state really. Georges wife of nearly fifty years, Freda, was sitting on the equally sad looking sofa. She was flicking through a magazine. It had been nearly a week, and neither one of them had spoken to the other. This was a way of life for them, ignoring each other when some silly misdemeanour had irritated either one or both of them. Probably now, they couldn't even remember what it was that had sparked yet another silence.

Meals were eaten in silence, and quite often prepared separately too. There was no one to tell them to stop acting like children. They were both without siblings and they had never had children of their own. When they met, as young people, they had plenty to say. They had hopes and dreams like all young lovers, and life had been good.

They both worked. George in the car industry and Freda had run a small dress shop. They enjoyed nice holidays a couple of times a year, and always went away for Christmas and New Year. Yes, life had treated them well. What changed? Nothing changed, they just got older and bored with each other. No more goals to achieve. Of course, life just plodded on, he pottered in the garden, she read her romantic novels. But they rarely spoke.

George got up from his tatty old chair and decided to inspect the garden before he made a cuppa for himself. She could get her own, he thought. He made his way out through the patio door into the back garden, and Freda didn't even look up from her magazine.

'Bloody 'ell, you damn silly animal. You nearly got trodden on.' George exclaimed, loud enough for Freda to look up to see what he was shouting about. 'It's that ruddy stray cat Freda,' shouted a rather irate George. 'Have you been feeding it again? I told you we'd never get rid of it if you did.'

'You old misery George' shouted Freda from the lounge, 'He's half starved, and you begrudge the poor defenceless animal a few morsels.'

'Defenceless my eye,' stated George. 'Blasted thing lies in wait for me to come out, then it dives underneath my feet. He'll have me over Freda, I'm telling you, he won't be satisfied until I've broken my neck.'

Freda laughed. 'Honestly George, you do have some funny ideas, he's just a hungry cat.' George was about to make a sarcastic comment, but he noticed, probably for the first time in ages, just how pretty Freda was when she laughed. Her eyes twinkled, just the same as they had when they were young, and in love. George realised that he couldn't remember the last time he had heard her laugh, or even when he had last laughed. Had things really got so bad between them?

George smiled and said, 'Well perhaps I do old girl, maybe I should find him something to eat, see if we can become friends. If he's going to be a regular visitor, I'd rather have him onside.'

Freda smiled back at George, and said. 'That's a good idea love, open a tin of tuna. I can make us a sandwich for tea with what's left.'

George went back inside and wandered into the kitchen with a skinny ginger tom following very close behind. 'Well Freda, don't think we'll be having tuna for tea, that poor cat was ravenous, he's eaten the lot.' George walked into the lounge and sat down in his chair. 'Suppose we ought to try and find out who he belongs to old girl.'

Freda said, in a sorrowful voice, 'I know who he belongs to George, it's that little family down the road, you know the one I mean, the lady died, left her husband and the little lad, and the cat of course.'

George looked a little puzzled, 'So why is the cat coming here then?' He asked. 'It's very sad George,' said Freda. 'The poor man isn't coping very well. They were only a young couple with a six-year-old boy. She got knocked down coming back from the shops, it's been a few months, but from what I've heard her husbands not doing so good.'

'Oh dear, that's a shame, maybe we could go and have a word with him, perhaps suggest we adopt the cat.' George thought he'd made a marvellous suggestion.

'GEORGE, it's the little boy's pet, we can't do that.' Freda stated crossly

'Well, what do you suggest?' George asked, and, somewhat patiently for him. Freda thought for a moment. 'I have an idea, get your coat George, we're popping out.'

'Where to? Shall I get the car?' He asked.

'No love,' said Freda. 'We are just going down the road.'

They stepped out of the front door of their small bungalow and pulled it shut. 'So where are we going?' George enquired, he wasn't much of a walker.

'Not far,' Freda answered, 'We're going to introduce ourselves to the cat owner'.

Cromwell Road was a nice little road. About twenty dwellings either side. Small, neat gardens fronted all of the houses and bungalows. It was clear that the residents all took pride in the appearance of their abode. 'Here we are,' said Freda. 'This is the house, number seventeen.' It had only been a two-minute walk.

The front garden was immaculate. There was no lawn, it was block-paving. There were a few plant pots dotted about, and it looked as though spring bulbs were beginning to grow inside them. That will look very pretty soon, thought George as he and Freda approached the front door.

Freda reached up and rang the doorbell. A young man answered the door fairly quick time. He was good-looking and sported the very fashionable facial stubble. 'Hello,' said Freda, ' You don't know us, but we are here about your cat.' The young man looked slightly worried. 'What about my cat?' He asked quietly.

Freda smiled, and said 'Don't look so worried, I just thought I should let you know that we have been feeding him. He visits us several times a day.'

'Oh, that's a relief, I thought for a moment you were going to tell me something awful had happened to him.'

The young man seemed quite upset. 'I don't know how I could have told my son his beloved pet had gone, he is still trying to get over losing his mum.'

Freda reached out and patted his hand, 'it can't be easy for you lad.'

He shook his head. 'No, it's hard, I don't know what I'm doing half the time. I am never sure how much food to give the cat, I don't know what Billy's favourite food is. I don't even know how much washing powder to put in the washing machine, my wife did everything.'

George had stood quietly by, just listening to the tale of woe. Suddenly he piped up. 'So, who is Billy? Is he your son, or your cat?' Freda looked at George and shook her head, then glanced at the young man stood in the doorway. He was actually smiling. 'Sorry, I have gone on a bit haven't I! Let me introduce myself.' He offered his hand to George. 'I'm Will Morgan, my son's name is Billy, and the cat is called Hector.'

George shook hands with Will, 'Lovely to meet you, son, I'm George Jacobs, and this is my other half, Freda.'

'Would you like to come in Mrs Jacobs, Mr Jacobs? Billy is inside watching C-Beebies.' Will said, then stepped aside to let the couple in. 'I will introduce you to Billy and then sort out what I owe you for feeding Hector.'

'Oh no, that's not why we came.' Freda was shocked to think Will thought they had come for payment for feeding Hector. 'George and I didn't know if you had family close by to help out sometimes, we thought that perhaps you would need a babysitter so you could go out with friends once in a while.'

'But you hardly know me, yet you would do this!' Stated Will. 'That's such a nice gesture.'

Freda smiled at him and said quietly, 'You need a break from your troubles once, in a while, we have no family, just the two of us. We have time on our hands. If we can help out, just ask. We live at number three, in one of the bungalows.'

Will put the kettle on, and the three of them sat in the very modern, red and white kitchen, and waited patiently for the kettle to boil. Over a cuppa, Will had explained to Freda and George that his late wife had been brought up by her grandparents and they were long gone. His parents had emigrated to Australia several years ago, so, it was just him and Billy, muddling on the best way they could.

The couple had met young Billy and were very impressed by the youngster's immaculate manners and winsome smile. He was a little shy at first, and Freda noticed sadness in his eyes. Poor lamb, she thought, so young and no Mummy.

Billy soon relaxed around the elderly couple, especially when George got down on the floor with him to build something with the building blocks. All too soon it was time to leave the Father and Son to their evening routine. It was Billy's bath-time, he had school the following day. But not before dates and times had been arranged for Billy to visit the couple for tea, and for them to go and babysit while Will took time out from being a single parent. Also, a promise that next Sunday, Will and Billy would go round to Freda and Georges for one of Freda's famous Sunday roasts. She hadn't done one in a while but was sure she hadn't forgotten how.

The elderly couple walked home hand in hand, smiling at one another. They were looking forward to being surrogate Grandparents to young Billy. Their lives had found purpose again, and they knew they were going to enjoy the next few years watching Billy grow.

As they walked in through the front door of their home, Freda turned to George and said, 'I think it's time to consider a new three piece suite George. Something a bit more modern, and perhaps child-friendly. After all, George, if we are going to have regular visits from our two boys we want them to be comfortable.'

'Couldn't agree more old girl, and I reckon a few toys from the charity shop for the lad to play with when he's here.'

'That's a grand idea George.' Said a delighted Freda. '

Tell you what,' said George. 'I will make us a cuppa, and we can sit at the table and make a list of everything we need.'

As he walked into the kitchen, George smiled to himself. That cat Hector has done us a favour, he thought. Life was going to be very busy in the little bungalow from now on. Silences were already a thing of the past.

The Coach Station

The ethnic woman with her braided hair and colourful attire stood in front of the locked glass door and stared at it. She leaned forward, then stared a bit more, almost as though she was willing it to open, but of course, that was never going to happen.

A young girl battled through the turnstile to the baby changing area. But how do you manoeuvre a huge suitcase, a rucksack, a pushchair complete with baby, and yourself, through something that only caters for the average size person? The poor girl appeared to be very harassed and looked as though she wished she was anywhere but there.

Meanwhile, people came in, and went out, of the coach station, dragging, or carrying, hold-alls and suitcases of every shape, size and colour. The ethnic lady moved onto another door, and another, and another. They all refused to open for her, even though her stare had become more intense. It had yet to dawn on her that the doors could only be opened from the other side.

Panic was setting in. She needed to be the other side of the doors. She only got off the coach to go to the loo. It was just a stop to pick up more passengers. What if it went without her. A courier stepped in front of the door and pressed a button. The door magically opened and she was able to go through the doorway and get back on her coach. The relief was visible on her face. No one knew she was going to her mothers funeral.

The young girl was now battling her way back from the baby-changing area. Why did no one offer a helping hand? She struggled once more, but she managed, - well, what choice did she have?

An elderly couple looked at a row of seats. Black, PVC coverings, ripped and torn. Well past their sell by date. The couple sat side by side and discussed the merits of the coffee shop situated at the far end of the coach station. They had half an hour to wait until their coach was due. Would they have a coffee? Or maybe it's cheaper to get a cold drink from the vending machine? After much deliberation, the vending machine won, and two bottles of Sprite were safely retrieved from the occasionally temperamental snack machine.

A Rastafarian stepped out from the disabled bathroom. He wasn't disabled, neither was he a traveller. He was a tree surgeon, and he was taking his lunch break. The quietly spoken young man explained to the elderly couple that he had nipped into the coach station to purchase coffee and a sandwich, but first needed to remove the bits of tree debris that were caught up in his clothing and his very long dreadlocks. He would return to work after lunch.

Two coaches pulled into the station simultaneously. People appeared from nowhere, and in true British fashion, formed an orderly queue in front of the closed glass doors. Meanwhile, passengers alighted from the two coaches and waited patiently for their baggage.

Once again a courier opens the glass doors. Bags are claimed, and the passengers move through the open doors and head towards the exits and waiting taxis.

Boarding the coaches is imminent for the orderly queue of people, and goodbyes are hastily said. The young girl with the baby is busy trying to fold down her pushchair with one hand, she is holding her baby with the other. Finally, someone offers a helping hand.

At the enquiries desk raised voices can be heard. A young girl is relating her tale of woe to a staff member. Her Dad would meet her the other end in Cardiff. She stated that 'He'll pay the fare.'

The staff could not authorise that, she was told. 'Get your Father to book you a ticket online.' The staff member stated, rather irately. 'There's still time.'

'HE WON'T DO THAT.' The young girl shouted. 'BUT I NEED TO GET BACK HOME, MY FATHER WILL BE STAMPING IF I'M NOT ON THE COACH!'

The staff member spoke abruptly. 'No ticket, no coach trip, sorry, but those are our rules.' The young girl sat on the floor and cried. Frustration? Maybe. Anger? Definitely. She was used to getting her own way. She needed to go home to Wales and had no money.

'Excuse me.' A businessman spoke to the young girl. 'I'd like to help, if I may.' He pushed two twenty pound notes into her hand. 'I have a daughter about your age, I would like to think someone would help her if she needed it. Go and get yourself a ticket.' The girl raised her tear stained face up to the man, gave a half-hearted smile and mumbled a thank you. He walked away, happy to know she would get home.

The young girl looked at the woman behind the desk. 'Ticket to Cardiff please,' and waved a twenty-pound note at her. 'Student rate.'

Children run around, and people come and go. Coaches come in and go out again, ferrying passengers to all four corners of the UK. The busy coach station is a multicultural waiting room. A place where people smile at each other (sometimes). Occasionally get angry, or help each other (eventually), and strike up conversations with complete strangers. A hive of activity that has the welcoming smell of coffee. People of all ages, and clothing styles and colours of several nations. An hour or two in this place is like living in a world we all want. Friendly, entertaining and busy.

Valentine's Day

Daisy had chosen her outfit very carefully this morning. She wanted everything to be perfect. Laid out on her bed was a pair of black jeans and a pink fluffy jumper. It was an outside date, and Daisy knew she needed to be warm. She hoped it wouldn't rain, she didn't really want to wear a coat.

She wondered to herself why Valentine's Day had to be in February. Why not in July or August when the weather was better? It was early, 9 00am. They weren't meeting till 10 30am. She wouldn't dress yet she thought, so instead, put her dressing gown on over her jim-jams and went downstairs for breakfast.

Eating her cereal, Daisy looked out of the window at the sky. It was a bit cloudy, but she could see some blue peeping through. Her mum would say there wasn't enough to make a sailor a suit, but there was enough blue up there to suggest it would stay dry. She glanced at the kitchen clock. 9 45am. A quick trip to the bathroom to clean her teeth and brush her long, honey-blonde hair, then, by the time she was dressed, it would be almost 10 30am. She didn't want to be late.

At last. The hall clock chimed on the hour, and the half hour, the melodic sound told Daisy it was time to go. She picked up her bag and went into the hallway, and out of the front door.

Daisy lived in a pretty little village, and her house was across the road from the village green with its little bandstand, ornate garden and a small duck pond. Daisy crossed over the road and sat on the bench close to the duck pond. Hopefully, she wouldn't have to wait too long.

Nick lay in bed, he knew time was moving on. It wouldn't take long to get dressed though, he'd get up in a minute. It was 9 45am. They said 10 30am. He could do that. Just five more minutes, quick shower and throw some clothes on. Yes, he'd be ready by 10 30am. No problem.

Daisy sat on the bench gazing around, she felt as though she had been waiting for ages, and then she spotted him. 'Thought you weren't coming.' Daisy stated. Without giving her an answer, he just smiled and took her hand. They walked to the edge of the duck pond. 'I brought bread,' said Daisy. 'I like feeding the ducks.' They stood, side by side and threw bits of bread into the pond. The ducks thought it was terrific, and splashed about in the water trying to reach the soggy treats.

Daisy blinked and smiled to herself. She had never forgotten her first Valentines Day date. Feeding the ducks with the boy next door. The date lasted all of half an hour. 14th February 1995. They were seven years old.

Today was 14th February 2018. 'Nick,' shouted Daisy, 'Are you getting up today? It's gone ten already, your tea is going cold.' Nick came bounding downstairs and into the kitchen where his wife was putting a fluffy pink coat on their two-year-old daughter Poppy. He was rubbing his hair dry with a towel. He reached for his mug of tea and drank it down in one go. Pulling a face at his wife, he said, 'Ugh, that was nearly cold.'

She laughed, and said, 'serves you right, you should get up in the mornings instead of lollygagging in bed.' Nick ran his fingers through his hair. That was all the combing it got that day or any other day for that matter. 'We can stop off at the roadside greasy Joes on our way. They do the best bacon butties, and, the tea's always hot.' Nick winked at Daisy.

'Cheeky devil,' said Daisy, smiling. 'The tea I make always starts off hot. Now come on, let's get going, or we'll never get there.'

They went there every Valentines Day. Back to the little village where they grew up together and where their parents still lived next door to each other. Where Daisy and Nick have fed the ducks every Valentines Day since they were seven years old. Of course, they visit their parents regularly, and the two doting sets of Grandparents take their little flower, Poppy, to feed the ducks. Valentines Day though, is just for Daisy and Nick, as it always has been for the last twenty-three years.

The Lavender Garden

The day was cold, damp and downright miserable. It was July, and fourteen-year-old Bunty Fielding was fed up. She was stuck in this depressing place until September. She had begged her parents not to send her to stay with Granny Fielding. 'It's not fair,' she cried. 'My friends get beach holidays, they get taken abroad. Why do I have to go to Granny's?'

Granny's was a very remote, and somewhat bleak area, in the back of beyond. Granny Fielding was a writer and always insisted she could only write in absolute peace and solitude, and for as long as Bunty could remember, she spent the whole of her summer holidays there. This time though, her two cousins, twins, Nicholas and Jack had been there too, and of course Mummy and Daddy and Aunty Jeannie and Uncle Harry (Daddies brother).

As youngsters, Bunty recalled the fun the three of them had, exploring, climbing trees and making dens. The sun always shone too, Bunty seemed to remember. This year the twins were both holidaying with friends in Cornwall. They would be living on Cornish pasties and cream teas, as well as learning how to surf, while Bunty was convinced she would see no such delights staying with Granny.

Mummy and Daddy were working to get a new business off the ground and couldn't take time out for a holiday, but they saw no reason for Bunty to miss her holiday too. Granny agreed to have Bunty to stay but would not be able to spend much time with her. She had a deadline to meet. Bunty would have to occupy herself.

Now here she was on this dreary July day feeling really fed up. Bunty only saw Granny at breakfast time and supper time. Granny didn't eat lunch. Bunty wasn't used to her own company, she had her friends back home, there was always someone to hang out with. She wasn't used to occupying herself. She wondered what she could do for the next two months to keep herself from going crazy.

Bunty wandered around the walled enclosure of the garden thinking to herself how much bigger it seemed when she was younger. The garden was a mess. Granny had long since ceased paying a gardener to keep it tidy. She looked around kicking at bits of broken pot lying on the overgrown pathway. There was bramble, already showing signs of taking over the whole garden, but the deep purple fruits were beginning to ripen. A bit of sun and the succulent blackberries would be ready for harvesting. If the sun ever bothers to visit here anymore, thought Bunty.

Gazing absentmindedly at the wall running down the left-hand side of the garden Bunty spotted a wooden door that she couldn't recall seeing before. She carefully made her way across the garden towards the heavy looking door, taking care not to get snagged on the brambles or brush against the nettles. The garden was like a botanical assault course. When Bunty reached the door that was set solidly in the wall, she saw immediately that it had a heavy, black, iron ring that almost looked like a door knocker. She put her hand through the ring and tried to turn it, hoping the door would open. It wouldn't.

Just below the ring was a keyhole, a large keyhole. The door was locked. Bunty decided she would ask Granny if she had a key and if so, she thought she might like to explore this new-found section of Granny's wilderness.

Bunty looked down at the watery offering that Granny called soup. She may well be a writer thought Bunty, she's certainly no cook. Bunty drank the soup anyway. Not entirely sure what it was meant to be, and too polite to ask. She was hungry.

Pudding proved to be a little better, fresh strawberries and ice cream. 'Granny?' Bunty thought now was as good a time as any to ask about the key to the door in the wall.

'What,' answered Granny, a little distracted.

'The door in the garden wall is locked. Do you have a key?'

'What door Bunty? There are no doors in the garden.' Stated Granny.

'Yes Granny, there is, it's in the wall on the left-hand side. I saw it.' Bunty spoke with some indignation.

Granny looked at Bunty and loudly said, 'OH, THAT DOOR! No Bunty, I do not have a key. Please keep away from it. There is nothing to interest you the other side of the wall.' Bunty was slightly taken aback by her grandmother's response, and in true teenage style, responded with a full blown tantrum. 'It's not fair, I'm so bored, am I just to twiddle my thumbs for the next two months? You don't care, nobody cares. This is my holiday, AND I'M BORED.'

Bunty flounced out, slamming the door behind her. Granny Fielding smiled. Just the response she expected, or, rather hoped for. If Bunty was the girl Granny thought she was, then she would find the key and pass through that door. Bunty sat on her bed crying tears of frustration. I'll show her, she thought. I will find a way in through that door. There has to be a way, or a key.

Bunty was awake bright and early the following morning. The weather looked considerably better than yesterday, and she was on a mission. One way, or another, she would see what was on the other side of the big wooden door. Bunty knew she had misbehaved at supper last night, so knocked on Granny's study door to apologise. 'Granny?' Bunty called out, knowing she dare not enter unless asked.

'WHAT DO YOU WANT BUNTY?' Yelled her granny.

'I just want to apologise for my behaviour last night Granny. I'm so sorry I was rude.'

'ACCEPTED, NOW GO AWAY. I AM VERY BUSY, AND BUNTY, ONE MORE THING.' Granny Fielding smiled to herself. 'STAY AWAY FROM THAT DOOR.'

Bunty thought to herself, not a chance, but answered, 'Yes Granny,' and headed to the kitchen to get breakfast. Obviously, Granny wouldn't be joining her this morning.

Bunty had yoghurt and banana, it was quick, and she was eager to get started on figuring out how she could open the door in the wall. The first thing Bunty did was to look through the keys hanging on a piece of wood in the scullery. There were lots of them to check. Granny Fielding hadn't made it too obvious when she hung the key to the big door amongst the others. But the big black key did stand out and she knew that her granddaughter wouldn't take too long to spot it amongst the smaller keys.

'Gotcha,' stated Bunty. She removed the key from its hook and stared at it. This has to be the key, Bunty thought as she headed out of the scullery.

Picking her way through the overgrown garden once more, Bunty couldn't wait to unlock the door and find out why Granny had told her to stay away. Finally reaching the big wooden door, reasonably unscathed from the brambles, but not entirely, Bunty pushed the key into the keyhole. She took a deep breath and turned the key.

The door opened very easily. Bunty had expected to find a little resistance, but no, the door swung open quite freely. What she saw the other side of the door was anything but what she expected. Buntys eyes opened wide in amazement, everywhere she looked was a carpet of purple. Every shade of purple you could imagine. The deepest, darkest plum colour, so dark it was almost black, to the palest mauve, so pale there was hardly any colour at all. Then there was the heady perfume. The smell was like walking into the biggest florist shop in the world.

'Ello Miss, what brings you this side of the wall? We don't often get visitors on this side.' Bunty jumped at the unexpected voice in her ear. She hadn't noticed anyone as she had opened the door, which had, she saw, shut behind her. 'Oh hello.' Bunty smiled at the old man who was now standing in front of her. 'Is it alright for me to be here?'

'Oh my word, yes, of course it is. I have been waiting a very long time for another visitor.' Answered the old man.

'The garden is wonderful, and, em, well, VERY purple,' stuttered Bunty.

The old man laughed, 'Yes it is.' Bunty stood in awe and just looked around her. The garden was much bigger this side of the wall, so neat, so weed free, so purple. Then Bunty looked up. The sky was the bluest she had ever seen. It was beautifully clear and free of even the whitest, fluffiest clouds, and the sun, like a big, golden sphere, shone brightly. The perfect summers day.

'I don't get it,' said Bunty to the old man, 'How can everything be so perfect? Why is this hidden behind the wall, and why haven't you tidied the other side?' Bunty couldn't work it out, she had so many questions she would be asking Granny at dinner tonight, even if it did get her into trouble for disobeying her Granny's wishes by coming into this side of the garden.

She looked at the old man and asked, 'Are you the gardener?'

'I am Miss.' He answered. 'Man and boy. The only garden I have ever tended, and,' he added, 'There is still a lot of work to be done.'

Bunty wondered to herself what could possibly need doing, it looked perfect. She also wondered how much more could the old gardener do. To her young eyes he looked at least a hundred years old already, shouldn't he be retired?

'Well young lady, do you have a name?' The old man asked. 'Or do you prefer me to call you Miss? I'm Ned.'

Bunty smiled. 'My name is Bunty, I'd rather that than Miss. Can I call you Ned?'

'Yes you may,' said Ned. 'Come on Bunty, I will show you around the garden, then we can have some lemonade in my potting shed. I'm sure I have some.'

The crazy paved garden paths were straight and not a weed to be seen in the cracks. The flower beds were all uniformly the same size, and square in shape. Each square housed flowers that were identical in colour in a solid block, or many different shades of purple in other blocks. This created a chequerboard effect.

Bunty and Ned wandered up and down the even paths admiring the flowers and their varying shades of purple. Occasionally, they would stop and admire a particularly pretty flower with a very dark purple petal and a centre of the palest lilac shade. There were variegated petals of every imaginable purple.

The flowers looked as though they had been hand-painted and the scents were individual to each flower. They were all different. When the pair reached the potting shed, Ned produced an old garden chair. He brushed off a few bits of moss and a cobweb and invited Bunty to sit. Ned himself sprung up, and perched on the end of the workbench he used as a potting table. He did so with the vigour of a much younger man.

'So, Bunty, what do you think of the garden?' Enquired Ned.

'I'm not sure,' answered Bunty. 'The flowers are all the same. I know they are different colours... kind of... but, they are all roses.

It's a rose garden.' Ned laughed.'Bless you, yes, you noticed. There is a reason for that. Let me explain.' Ned told Bunty that her Great Great Grandmother was a keen gardener but the only flowers she really liked were Lavender and Roses. Sadly the soil wasn't suitable to grow Lavender. She tried many times but always failed. She hired gardener after gardener who didn't seem to realise that the heavy clay-like soil just wasn't what Lavender needed. Then Ned was employed as an apprentice. He soon noticed that while the Lavender would not grow in the heavy soil, the Roses were thriving. Ned explained to Bunty that Roses were not so fussy about the soil they grew in, as long as it drained well.

As the years went by, Great Great Grandmother recognised the growing skills of Ned, and how he tended her garden with love and pride. She had a section of the garden walled off and set a task for Ned. Ned carried on explaining to Bunty precisely what that task was.

'Your Great Great Grandmother asked me to produce a rose that has the smell of Lavender. She always knew that it would never happen in her lifetime, but she hoped, that eventually, there would be a Lavender Garden here. Albeit, not the Lavender shrub she loved, but the beautiful scent that it produces.'

Bunty was transfixed listening to Ned's story. 'Have you done it, Ned?' Bunty was keen to know. 'No, Bunty, I'm still trying, and I will keep trying until I succeed.' Answered Ned. 'I am close, but not quite close enough.'

Bunty wondered about the time, she felt as though she had been with Ned all day. She decided she had better go and face the music, once Granny knew where Bunty had been she would be cross. She obviously would be very annoyed knowing that Bunty had disturbed Ned's work. Bunty said goodbye to Ned and said she hoped she would see him again before her holiday ended. She slipped through the big wooden door, locking it behind her.

As she once more picked her way through the bramble ravaged garden, Bunty wondered where the entrance was for Ned to enter and leave the Rose Garden. Bunty went straight to the kitchen to replace the key in the scullery. Just in time thought Bunty, as Granny walked in.

'Ah, there you are Bunty, are you all packed? Your parents will be here soon.'

'Am I going home Granny?' Asked Bunty.

'Yes Bunty, holidays don't last forever.' Responded her Granny.

'Well, this one certainly hasn't.' Said Bunty.

Granny poured Bunty a glass of milk and reached for the biscuit tin. 'Come on Bunty, you and I need a little chat.'

Bunty followed her Granny into the lounge. Granny explained to Bunty that she knew she had been through the big wooden door into the Rose Garden, just as she expected her to do. What Bunty didn't know was that she also walked into a time warp. What felt like a few hours to Bunty, was, in fact, a whole two months on this side of the wall.

'But how? What causes it? When did it happen?' Bunty had so many questions. Granny smiled and said she hadn't got the answers to Bunty's questions.

'I don't know Bunty, I don't think we are supposed to know why or how.' Granny said, 'I was your age when I went through the door and met Ned and heard his story about my Great Grandmother and her dream of a Lavender Garden. I can only say, that like you, I was holidaying here with my Grandmother and my holiday passed by while I was with Ned. No one seems to be able to explain it. My Grandmother couldn't any more than I can, and I suspect no more than you will be able to when your granddaughter passes through the door.

'Then just how old is Ned, Granny?' His age intrigued Bunty.

'I can only tell you that he's probably much, much older than he looks, and I am not sure what will happen if he finally produces a perfect rose that smells of lavender.'

Granny also added, when, and only when, the Lavender Garden is complete, and the pleasant smell of lavender permeates the whole garden, will the wall come down and the garden once more become as one again. 'I suppose,' said Granny, 'That I should really get the garden sorted on this side of the wall. Maybe its time to employ a gardener again? Now off you go young lady, get your bag packed.'

'Granny, when was the last time Ned had a visitor?' He said it was a very long time.'

'It was Bunty, it was me when I was the same age as you. His next visitor will be your Granddaughter, and you will have one.' Granny seemed most definite about that.

Sitting in the back of her parent's car, Bunty was in reflective mood. She knew she wouldn't see Ned again, or the Rose Garden and that she would never go through the big wooden door a second time. She hoped though that she would live long enough to smell the lavender scented roses and get to wander around her Great, Great Grandmothers much longed for Lavender Garden.

The Waiting Room

I am sitting here with my book, but in all honesty, it won't get opened, never mind a few lines actually read. It's busy here today. I say busy, but how would I know? I never come here. This could be a quiet day for all I know.

The last time I was in this waiting room was a Saturday morning in October last year, for my flu jab. I watch the receptionist and wonder why she is actually here. The phone rings, and rings. She doesn't answer it, it is obviously meant to be answered by the infernal machine we have come to detest. Finally, the ringing stops. The machine has probably answered the poor unsuspecting patient by now and will be busy telling them their options. All they want is, hopefully, to get a doctor to see the boil on their bum. Will they care if by pressing three on their keypad they get through to the practice secretary, or by pressing five, they can speak to the cleaner. Joy of joys, they will also be asked, ' Did you know that you can now make or cancel a doctors appointment online?'

These methods are fine for the majority, but where is the consideration for they who are hard of hearing or visually impaired?. Where do they fit in?

Back to the 'busy' receptionist. She is sat shuffling papers now. She does speak, I spoke to her on my arrival. 'I have an appointment at...' That was as far as I got.

'Book yourself in over there please.' She said this as she was pointing to a square box on the wall. It's technology gone mad. Key your name in, and date of birth. The machine informed me, you have an appointment booked at 11 15 am with Doctor Cottings. Yes I know I do. I made the appointment myself.

Two elderly women sitting next to me, are discussing the merits of a lady doctor, who appears to be nameless. 'Oh, she's marvellous, very thorough, I was in with her for ages, much longer than I should have been.' The elderly lady laughed. 'Bet my name was mud out here.'

Her companion chortled, 'Oh Edna, and you with the constitution of an ox.'

'I'm getting fed up waiting now Hilda, I don't mind telling you,' stated Edna. 'These doctors, don't know why they have an appointment system. I'm already nearly ten minutes over my appointment time.' She huffed and puffed a bit. 'Not that I blame the doctors Hilda, Oh no, it isn't their fault. I blame selfish patients. No consideration for those sat waiting.' Hilda and Edna looked at each other and shook their heads.

'Mrs Johnson to room two please, Mrs Johnson to room two.' A phantom voice calls out from a small speaker high above our heads. Everyone looks up, what do we expect to see I wonder. Edna stands up and heads towards the corridor and room two. I glance at my watch and wonder how many appointment times she will encroach upon this time.

I'm getting bored now, I reach into my bag to retrieve my book. Just as I pull the book out from the black hole that is my handbag, the waiting room door flies open and a large, irate, middle-aged man, storms in and marches straight to the reception desk. The book is immediately dropped back into the dark depths, it looks as though the receptionist is about to start earning her wages.

'WHAT DO YOU PEOPLE ACTUALLY DO?' The middle-aged man yelled at the receptionist. She wasn't given a chance to respond before he launched into another tirade. 'YOU NEVER ANSWER THE PHONE, THERE IS NO HUMAN CONTACT. THERE MIGHT AS WELL BE A MONKEY SAT WHERE YOU ARE SITTING.'

'Do you have an appointment, Mr Er, um?' The receptionist whimpered. 'ME NAME ISN'T ER-UM, IT'S BILLINGSLEY, AND NO, I DO NOT HAVE AN APPOINTMENT. I WAS

PHONING TO MAKE ONE BUT KEPT GETTING THAT RUDDY MACHINE.' He emitted a fine spray of spittle from his mouth, it showered the unfortunate receptionist. She leaned back in a vague attempt to avoid the watery missile but failed miserably. She reached for a tissue.

'Mr Billingsley, since you are here now, would you like to make an appointment?' 'NO MADAM, I WOULD NOT.' Boomed the incensed Mr Billingsley. 'I AM BETTER NOW. I WANTED TO SEE A DOCTOR LAST WEEK WHEN I WAS ILL.'

Hilda looked at me and raised her eyebrows. 'Well, he does have a point,' she said. The receptionist rapidly tried to regain her composure as Mr Billingsley turned and stomped out of the building. I smiled to myself, it had obviously not been a problem with his vocal cords.

'Miss Thomas room five please, Miss Thomas room five.' Once again, we all look up. I stand up and begin to make my way towards room five. As I do, the phone rings. 'Good morning, Mason Road Surgery, how may I help you?' The receptionist was very quick off the mark. I wonder why? Maybe she is learning.

Embrace

For Sale... One Boa Constrictor. All essential equipment needed will be included in the price. Any reasonable offer considered. Genuine reason for selling. Tel. 0774776.

Calvin Alan Knott read the advert in his local newspaper with great interest. He checked the pet section every week, feeling certain that one day something other than furry kittens and skittish hamsters would be offered for sale. Today was that day.

Not wanting to miss this golden opportunity Calvin reached for his phone and immediately rang the number.

Calvin was an unusual young man who lived in the granny flat situated at the bottom of his parents rather large garden. He was 23 years old and was almost independent. His mother Dora provided his meals, she did his laundry and she cleaned his flat. Calvin's father, George, was a retired bank manager who didn't take much interest in his son. He thought he was a rather dull individual and preferred to spend time on the golf course, or more specifically, the 19th hole, discussing the state of the country with fellow golfers.

At a very early age Calvin found out that life could be cruel. His parents insisted on calling him Calvin Alan instead of just Calvin which he would have preferred. It wasn't long after he started school that his peers soon realised that his initials spelt CAK. For the rest of his school life he was known as Cak and toilet humour followed him wherever he went.

One certain individual, Jake Summers, made sure that Calvin, or Cak, never knew a moments peace. 'Is that cak I can smell?' Jake always shouted; he loved to be heard. 'Pooh, what's that stink? Oh, it's you Cak, thought you must be close by.'

Jake laughed, he thought he was very funny. Needless to say, poor unfortunate Calvin did not. As if going through school with the mean-spirited Jake Summers wasn't enough. Calvin found himself working with him, or rather for him.

Jakes father owned a garden centre. Simply called Summers Garden Centre but with the rather salacious slogan. We service your needs Winter, Spring and Autumn too. A cardboard cut out of a scantily dressed girl holding a large watering can bearing the slogan, was situated at the entrance to the garden centre. It was also on posters positioned around the building.

Calvin's job was rather menial, it was basically to keep the plants watered and to make sure that the centre was tidy. He was never trusted to serve customers. Jake on the other hand swanned around the place like he owned it, which of course one day, he would.

'Cak,' Jake would shout, 'These plants are drier than the Sahara, get them watered.' His people skills left a lot to be desired. Calvin had worked at the garden centre for five years and quite frankly, he'd had enough. Calvin had half a day off every other Tuesday and didn't work Sundays. Each Sunday morning was spent in church with his mother .A good, God fearing woman.

Today was Tuesday and Calvin was going to collect, and pay, for the Boa Constrictor he had seen advertised for sale in the local rag. He set off in a white van borrowed from a member of the congregation in church. Calvin knew the cage that housed the snake was ten feet long. The snake herself named Embrace, shortened to Em, was at least five foot long.

Calvin parked the van outside the house at the address, which had been given over the phone. Inside Calvin was securing the deal with the man selling the snake. He was selling because the snake had appeared to take a liking to the man's girlfriend and there had been a couple of close calls whereby the snake had nearly throttled her.

The seller said he thought it was her smell that attracted the snake, but did not continue with the conversation. Calvin had offered the man five hundred pounds for Embrace and her abode.. plus extras. The extras included, a water bowl, a rubber water bath so Em could soak when she wanted to, thermometer and lights, heat lamps and such, so that perfect living conditions could be maintained.

The man seemed happy with the price and even gave Calvin a supply of frozen food with the instructions to thaw before feeding. Food included frozen gerbils, guinea pigs and small rabbits. The two men struggled to get everything into the back of the van. Everything was very heavy. Embrace was in a black sack for the journey, this was to keep her calm. She couldn't travel in her cage, that was in sections and would have to be put together in Calvin's granny flat.

Calvin had given no thought to how he would manage to remove everything from the van, and get it indoors single-handedly. It had taken two of them to carry Em in her sack. Five-foot Boa Constrictors were not the lightest of reptiles. Then there was the rest of the paraphernalia.

Calvin arrived home as dusk was falling. He had a gargantuan task ahead of him. There was no way he could possibly get everything in-situ on his own. Only one thing for it thought Calvin, his parents would need to be called upon to lend a hand.

George wasn't so keen to help, but cajoled by his wife Dora, he soon gave in and proved to be very helpful. In little or no time the cage was reconstructed and everything was in place and ready for Em to move back in. Calvin's mum was not too keen on a snake being her sons pet, but his father thought it was marvellous and he began to view his son a little differently. Not as dull as he thought.

Over the following few days Em had settled quite nicely into her new surroundings and seemed none the worse for her travels. Calvin's mum, soon relaxed in her sons flat when she could see the dreaded reptile couldn't actually get out... She was happy to carry on with her cleaning and tidying of Calvin's home.

George was quite intrigued by his sons pet, and seemed to spend a lot more time in the evenings getting to know more about Em, and even his son, who seemed quite knowledgeable about Boa Constrictors. Em was a Red Tailed Boa, Calvin informed his father.

Em had been with Calvin about a week when he decided to invest in a large chest freezer. Mr Summers, Jakes father, had told Calvin that he could use his staff discount to purchase Ems frozen food from the pet section of the nursery. Of course, the more he bought, the cheaper it would be.

This made sense to Calvin. Jake had to deliver the frozen foodstuff to Calvin's home. There seemed, to Jake, an awfully large amount of frozen food for one snake that only got fed every few days. But still, Cak had coughed up and it was all money in the family coffers thought Jake.

Jake being Jake, he got Cak to carry most of the boxes. They were heavy, and Jake was lazy. Once the boxes were all inside the granny flat the two men set about putting them in the freezer. Again Jake left most of the work to Cak. Jake was too busy studying Em..

'Well' said Jake. 'You have certainly surprised me Cak, thought you were a right anorak, but a snake this size as a pet, I'm impressed.'

Cak heard himself saying to Jake, 'If you want to come round one evening, I can get Em out and you can get to know her, only if you want to of course.'

Jakes response was a surprise to Cak. 'Ace mate, I'd love to, shall I bring a bottle of something?'

Calvin smiled, 'That would be nice Jake, but don't you drive?' Jake said he'd walk to Calvin's and it was agreed he would visit on Friday evening, and maybe even send out for a Chinese meal.

Calvin had told his mother about his plans and she said she would give the place an extra spruce up, after all, it was his bosses son who was visiting.

Friday soon came around and once home from work, and Calvin changed from his logo bearing work clothes into a new shirt and his jeans. He then flipped the catches on Ems cage. At precisely 7 30pm Jake knocked on Calvin's door. 'Hello mate,' greeted a very amiable Jake, and handed Calvin two rather inferior bottles of red wine. Jake figured that Cak wouldn't have much clue about fine wines.

'Come in' invited Calvin, leading Jake into the lounge. 'Take a seat.' Ems cage sat behind the settee and Calvin dropped the glass front down leaving the cage open. 'She will come out in her own good time' said Calvin. 'She likes to stretch herself out across the back of the settee.' Calvin then left Jake and went to fetch some glasses for the wine. When Calvin returned to the lounge Em had come out of her cage and was indeed stretched out along the back of the settee. Well, almost stretched out, her tail section was coiled very firmly around Jakes neck. Jake was a rather fetching shade of purple, his lips were blue and his eyes were protruding from their sockets. It was quite clear to Calvin that Jake was dead.

Calvin allowed himself a wry smile. He knew that was what would happen because it had worked the night before on his father George. Calvin stroked the top of Ems head and she uncoiled her tail section from around Jakes neck. Once free of the heavy snake, Jake slumped forward. Calvin held a thawed out gerbil in front of Em and her tongue flicked in and out as she caught the scent of her food. Calvin placed the gerbil in Ems cage and she slithered back inside to eat her meal. Calvin then closed up the front and flicked the catches back in place. He then went into the kitchen and opened the freezer. He removed several boxes of Ems food until he could just see the frozen arm of his father draped around the body of his frozen mother. She had proven very difficult to kill because of course he couldn't leave Em to come out of her cage.

Dora wouldn't set foot in his home unless the snake stayed put. He made the decision to hit her over the head with a green onyx vase that sat on the sideboard. It worked. He placed his parents, facing each other in the very bottom of the freezer. Jake was going on top of them. Jake was a dead weight, but Calvin was no weakling and he soon had him in the kitchen.

Calvin got Jake upright and leaned him against the large freezer. As this was his third victim he now had what he had to do down to a fine art. As Calvin pushed Jake on his shoulder and tilted him back, he was able to sweep his legs up and topple him into the freezer. He landed with a crash on top of George and Dora. Calvin replaced all of the frozen snake food and covered up his victims. He slammed the freezer shut. 'Well Em, that's that.' Said Calvin to his pet,' They have made my life a misery between them. Not anymore.'

Calvin sat down and phoned the Shanghai Palace Chinese Takeaway, and then he ordered a meal. A meal for one.

The Turtle Stone

The young boy opened his eyes to unfamiliar surroundings. He sat up and rubbed his nose, something he always did if he was perplexed or a little unsure of something. He looked around, his eyes squinting in the brightness. 'Hello, sleepyhead.' The young boy smiled as he looked up into the smiling face of his Gran. 'Grandpa got fed up waiting for you to wake up young man,' his Gran said, laughing. 'He has taken the nets down to the brook. I hope he hasn't caught all of the newts and sticklebacks while you were sleeping. You had better get yourself to the brook toot sweet, I will come and join you when I have tidied away the picnic things.'

Ten-year-old Ben Giles took off like a Jackrabbit towards the brook, his blonde hair shining in the sunlight. Ben loved spending time with his Grandparents, but since last summer it hadn't happened very often. This was a rare treat indeed, and one he intended to make the most of. He was very cross with himself that he has fallen asleep. He couldn't even remember eating his picnic lunch, he wasn't feeling hungry though.

Like every ten-year-old boy, he was always hungry, so he must have eaten he told himself. Ben soon reached the brook and of course, Grandpa. The brook was only a few inches deep and as clear as tap water. Looking down into the sparkling water Ben could see the shoals of small fishes darting about. Small newts clambered over the smooth, shiny stones and, resting on the surface of the very gently flowing water was some frogspawn.

'There you are Ben, I was beginning to think you were never coming.' Ben's white-haired Grandpa was standing, ankle deep in the cool, clear water. Small fishes were swimming all around him. 'Come on get those shoes and socks off and join me for a paddle.'

Ben looked at his Grandpa and smiled. He did look funny with his trousers rolled up to his knees. In no time at all Ben was standing next to Grandpa and they were both slowly dragging their fishing nets through the water to see what they could catch. Gran had thoughtfully provided each of them with an empty jam jar and had tied a string around the top to make them easier to hold. Grandpa had explained to Ben that it was nice to catch the newts and the sticklebacks. Watching them in the water was lovely, but seeing them close up in the jam jar was better. They could see the colours clearer and all of their little details. The newt's tiny hands, and the orange spots on his belly, the sticklebacks broad tail fin and his lack of scales. 'But,' reminded Grandpa, 'Always put them back in the water as soon as you can. It's cruel to keep them in the jar for too long.' Ben promised his Grandpa he would always try to be kind to all creatures.

They carried on dredging with their nets, not saying a lot, just enjoying each others company. Grandpa broke the silence. 'There are turtles in these waters Ben.'

Ben looked at Grandpa and laughed, then said. 'There aren't.'

'Let me show you.' Said, Grandpa. He opened his hand, and as Ben looked at Grandpas open palm, he laughed again. There nestling in his hand was a small stone. It was just like a turtle. 'I found it in the stream while I was waiting for you,' said Grandpa with a smile.

'Can I keep it please Grandpa?' Asked Ben. 'I have just the place for it in my bedroom.'

'Of course, you can Ben,' answered his Grandpa.

'Yoo-hoo boys' called Gran as she came towards them. 'Soon be time to go'. Grandpa looked disappointed that time has gone so fast. As Ben turned to speak to his Gran, he slipped and plunged lengthways into the sparkling brook banging his head on a rock.

Ben opened his eyes and immediately rubbed his nose. He blinked and saw his Mum. She was standing over him, tears streaming down her face. 'Thank goodness Ben, we've been so worried about you, you are in the hospital. Can you remember what happened?'

'Yes,' answered Ben, 'I was catching newts and sticklebacks with Grandpa, I fell over in the stream.' Ben's Mum looked worried. 'No Ben, that isn't what happened. You got knocked off your bike going to school, you banged your head on the kerbstone. I'm just glad you were wearing your bicycle helmet otherwise things could have been a whole lot worse.' Ben looked puzzled. 'But Mum, I went on a picnic with Gran and Grandpa.'

Ben's Mum took his hand and said gently, 'Sweetheart, you can't have been on a picnic with them, they both died last year. I think you must have been dreaming about them after you bumped your head.' Ben's eyes filled with tears. He missed his Grandparents very much.

Several years later Ben had a last look around his room. He was off to university. His eyes were drawn to the small stone on his desk. Ben picked it up and smiled at the 'turtle stone' he held in his palm, just as his Grandpa had on the day he had given it to Ben. There was no explanation for what really occurred that summers day so long ago, but Ben knows he spent one day with his Grandparents that he shouldn't have had. He knows it wasn't a dream, and the little 'turtle stone' was all the proof he needed. Heaven had sent his Grandparents back to him for just a short while, maybe to make sure he stayed earthbound. Ben slipped the stone into his pocket. He was going nowhere without it.

Followed

She heard the twig snap behind her, for one brief moment, her heart stopped beating. She was sure someone was following her.

Mandy Fellowes had been to visit a client who lived at the far end of a narrow lane in the village of Benton. She parked her car in the car park of the local pub and walked the short distance to her client's cottage. Mandy was a mobile hairdresser, and she visited the elderly Mrs Jackson every six weeks to trim her hair.

The village was a little out of the way for Mandy, but Mrs Jackson was a sweet old lady, and housebound. Mandy was a caring, and considerate young woman and didn't mind putting herself out for the old lady. She always stayed longer than necessary sharing a cuppa and a gossip, and Mrs Jackson still enjoyed Mandy's visits. The only fly in the ointment for Mandy was Mrs Jackson's son. He lived with his mother, and he made Mandy feel very uncomfortable.

Mandy always felt as though the middle-aged man was watching her. He rarely spoke, but when he did it was usually to ask if she had a boyfriend, or to tell her what a pretty girl she was. It was later than ever this evening when Mandy had left Mrs Jacksons, and it was getting dark. Mandy quickened her step, she could see her car in the pub car park and just wanted to reach it, get in, and drive home. She reached her car, unlocked it and sat inside. She locked the doors, then searched inside her handbag, foraging for her mobile phone. A quick phone call to her car mechanic boyfriend of eight months would calm her jangling nerves.

Gary Thompson answered his phone on the first ring. 'Hello love, you ok'?

'No, I'm not Gary, I'm a nervous wreck'. Mandy sounded close to tears. 'I think Mrs Jackson's son followed me back to my car, he gives me the creeps. I'm sure he was following me down the lane'.

Gary laughed, 'Oh I'm sure he wasn't. Why would you think that?'

Mandy snapped at Gary. 'Because he's always staring at me, and saying things, that's why'.

'OK, I'm sorry, he's obviously bothered you'. Gary sounded contrite, 'I didn't mean to upset you. Are you alright to drive back'?

'Yes, I think so, I'll be fine'. Mandy sounded a little calmer.

'I will meet you at the pizza place, if I'm not there, wait for me', said Gary. 'I have a few bits to finish at the garage, but I shouldn't be too long'.

They said goodbye and Mandy started her car, as she pulled out of the pub car park she glanced in the mirror and saw Mrs Jackson's son stood at the end of the lane, watching her.

Mandy arrived at the pizza restaurant and couldn't see Gary. She decided to sit in her car and wait for him to come. Usually, she would do a little window shopping if she was waiting. Tonight was different. The business with Mrs Jackson's son had unsettled her, and she felt happier locked inside her car. This wasn't the first time Mandy thought she was being followed, there had been other times when she suspected she was. Tonight was the first time she had mentioned it to Gary though.

At first, she thought it was her imagination, she never actually saw anyone, but just sensed that someone was almost stalking her. But now, now was different because she saw Mrs Jackson's son at the end of the lane. He must have followed her.

Gary turned up several minutes later, and they agreed to have their pizza boxed, and they would go home and eat it. Mandy wasn't in the mood to sit in the restaurant. Home for the young couple was a one bedroom flat in the high street. The building used to be the old rent offices but the council had spent taxpayers money on a new office block. The rent offices were converted into a block of four flats.

Mandy had moved in with Gary three months ago. Everyone who knew them said it was far too soon, but they were very happy and determined to prove the doubters wrong. Everything would be perfect if it were not for the fact that Mandy was convinced she was being followed.

As the days and weeks moved along, there had been several occasions when Mandy had told Gary that she had been followed again. 'I would tell you to go to the police Mandy', Gary shouted, 'But what the hell would that achieve? You have no proof, you never see anyone'. She knew Gary was right, if he didn't believe her, how could she possibly convince anyone else, especially the police.

Gary's patience was wearing thin, Mandy was starting to think she was imagining things, and on top of that Mrs Jackson would be expecting her to go and trim her hair again that evening. 'Come with me, Gary'. Mandy begged, 'Mrs Jackson is always saying she'd like to meet you'.

'I can't, I'm sorry love, I promised a customer I would tow his car to the garage. I can't go until he gets in from work himself. I did tell you'. Gary was very apologetic.

'Oh yes, I forgot', said Mandy. In honesty, Mandy couldn't remember Gary telling her, but she was always so distracted these days, she was barely functioning at all.

'Perhaps you should cancel', suggested Gary, though he knew Mandy wouldn't let the old lady down.

'No I won't do that, she likes me visiting, it's not her fault she has a pervy son'. Mandy was quite indignant at Gary's suggestion.

All too soon the time arrived when Mandy had to return to the village of Benton. She gathered up her case and checked she had her scissors, combs and brushes. As Mandy drove she wondered to herself if she could maybe drive her car up the lane to Mrs Jacksons cottage. Realistically she knew that the lane was far too narrow for any vehicle. She had no option other than park in the pub car park, as always, and walk there.

When Mandy arrived at the cottage, she took a deep breath and knocked on the door. 'Come on in lovey', shouted Mrs Jackson. 'It's open'.Mandy pushed open the front door and went through into the kitchen where Mrs Jackson was sat ready and waiting for her.

The teapot was sat on the table underneath a knitted tea cosy, and there were four custard creams on a tea plate; two china mugs finished off the table setting. As neither took sugar in their tea, there was no sugar bowl, and the milk was in the fridge.

'Will you be mother, dear'? Asked Mrs Jackson.

'Of course I will', laughed Mandy, and turned to get the milk from the fridge. Once the tea had been drunk and biscuits eaten, Mandy trimmed Mrs Jackson's hair.

It was still relatively light outside, and Mandy was determined to leave Mrs Jackson before darkness fell. 'You have probably noticed my son isn't here today, he's gone to meet a friend at the pub, he doesn't get out much', stated Mrs Jackson. Mandy had realised he wasn't home but was worried that he may come back before she left. 'Will he be out late'? Asked Mandy.

'Probably not', answered Mrs Jackson. Mandy glanced at her watch, six fifteen p.m. She informed Mrs Jackson that she had to go because she had another appointment. It wasn't strictly true, but she wanted to leave before Mrs Jackson's son returned from the pub.

Mandy said goodbye to Mrs Jackson and headed off down the lane. She hadn't gone very far when she saw Mrs Jackson's son walking towards her. Mandy could feel herself starting to panic, she was convinced this man meant her harm.

'Mandy, I need to talk to you, it's about that mechanic chap, he follows you everywhere'. Mrs Jackson's son was shouting up the lane to Mandy.

'Go away', Mandy screamed, 'Leave me alone'. Mandy saw an opening in the hedge to the right of her. She turned and ran into a small wooded area. 'Mandy'. The voice calling was quite close, but Mandy didn't hear it clearly enough to recognise it. The blood was pounding in her ears, and her heart was beating loudly like a drum.

A hand grabbed her and spun her around. 'Gary thank goodn'......... Mandy stopped mid-sentence and watched in horror as he raised his arm up above his head. He was holding a car jack in his hand. As Gary lowered his hand, the car jack was the last thing Mandy ever saw.

Surprise

I hate surprises, no, I really mean it, I hate surprises. The last time someone surprised me, I wet myself. Now, this may be perfectly acceptable if you are four years old, and someone shouts boo in your face. When you are a forty something P.A., it isn't quite as acceptable. It wasn't even a big surprise. Well, it was... My boss decided to surprise me with a hazelnut latte and a crispy creme doughnut. Why? Because I had been his P.A. for five years.

The day started like any other, I was running late, that's the norm. I always miss the bus, I'm sure it comes earlier than it should. I then have to walk to the train station. You guessed it, I missed my train too. Inevitable really. That happens every day as well. Public transport, so unreliable!!!

I always get to work, eventually. I'm not usually too late. Anyway, as I was saying, the day started like any other. I certainly had no reason to think it would be any different to my usual working day. It wasn't, not to begin with. I always start the day with coffee for Fred and me.. Fred's my boss. The company? See Clear Windows.

We have one of those vending machines that dispense hot drinks and soup, it's down in the foyer. I say foyer, I think I mean the gap by the entrance as we walk in. Anyway, that's where I get the coffee from. I think it's coffee, its the same colour as the oxtail soup smells a tad wrong for coffee, but it's usually wet and warm, and with an added sweetener it's drinkable. Fred never complains about it.

Back to the day in hand, I do tend to go off on a tangent sometimes. You will get used to it, and I always get to the point, at some stage. I had got the coffees from the machine on my way in, as I always do. Then went straight to the office. Up three flights of stairs. No lift, so I have to walk up. They do say it's very good for you. Must say, I have calves of steel. My knees, however, well that's a different story.

I will just tell you this though, you can hear me coming. My knees are very creaky. Anyhow, as I was saying, I went straight to the office and, as I do any other morning, popped into Fred's office and placed his coffee on the desk. He's never there. Always comes in after me. Think he must have the same problem with public transport that I have. His must come too early as well. He will arrive before the coffee gets cold though, he always does.

It's not a big company, just three of us. It's five if you count the two men who fit the windows. I tend not to count them because Fred rarely sells any windows. The men are only called upon when needed. The last time I recall seeing them was November 2015. Think we must have had an offer on that month. Mr and Mrs Farley-Charles bought a kitchen window and two bedroom windows. Not sure why they only needed three windows, I probably didn't ask. I imagine you are quite impressed though, at my remarkable memory, after all, this did happen two years ago.

It's not so difficult, Fred hasn't sold a window since, and who could forget a name like Farley-Charles. As I was saying before my tangent interfered again. There are only three of us, though technically speaking it is really just two of us. Me and the boss. The third person is the cleaner, but she's on long-term sick. Hasn't been seen in months.

Brunhilda Weiss (pronounced Vice.) Isn't German, or Austrian or Swiss. She just thinks she is. She was just plain Hilda Stanley until she met, and married Archie Weiss who comes from Wigan. Someone made the mistake of asking if he was German, or Austrian, or indeed Swiss. Hilda immediately saw the glamour in this possibility and promptly wrote Brun in front of Hilda and became Brunhilda. She then developed an accent to match her name. On her last day at work, before her 'sickness' really kicked in, she said to me, 'Leeby,' (my name is Libby). She said, 'Leeby, my legs don't vant to valk the steps no more. I vant to vork somevere flat. I vill valk out today and not return.' She did just that.

Religiously, every Monday morning Archie rings and informs us that, 'Our Brunhilda won't be in again this week, 'Ers still feeling a bit off.' It seems to have passed by unnoticed that she is working in an Austrian teashop. I have frequented the place several times. She hasn't lost her accent but struggles with some words. Her northern roots have turned Baumkuchen into Bumcookin, and Kirschtorte into Kitchtorty, but she tells me she's keeping, 'Very vell Leeby.'

So, having introduced you to the workforce, I will explain my duties as a P.A. and what my work entails. A simple description is, I don't really do very much at all. Fred deals with sales, so he doesn't do much either. I answer the phone if it rings. It rings more now than it used to. Quite a boon these cold callers, or telesales to be more precise. I have some good long chats with the ones trying to sell double glazing. I pick their brains a bit and pass on a few tips to Fred. Who knows, it may get us another sale one day.

P.P.I. That's another good one, surprising how a conversation can be stretched if you answer the questions. It all passes the time away. Filing. I do quite a lot of filing. There are several different filing systems. I do them all throughout a few weeks. Just for something to do really. Then there's the computer. I did a little course, well, Fred insisted. It's marvellous, I can't do anything work related on it, I don't understand any of it, but Facebook is terrific, I traced a couple of school friends too, and I can play all sorts of games. Wonderful invention. Makes work very pleasurable.

Cleaning. I do that too since Brunhilda left us high and dry. I flick a duster over the desks and windowsills, and once a week I run around with the hoover. I don't plug in or switch it on. No point, it's broken. I do literally take it out of the cleaning cupboard and run around the office with it. It's all exercise, isn't it? I have told Fred it's broken, but he says it's an unnecessary expense. He's not wrong, floors look ok in the right light.

That's it really, not much more I can tell you. Oh, I nearly forgot, I was going to tell you about my surprise wasn't I! Fred had popped out, he sometimes does. Not really sure why. Anyway, he went off with his usual cheery, 'Bye Miss Borabarovski, see you later.' That's my name.. Elizabeth (Libby) Ermentrude Borabarovski. I have asked him to call me Libby, but he says its more professional if he calls me Miss Borabarovski. It's such a mouthful. I have often wondered why my mother couldn't have married a man called Smith, oh well.

Anyway, yet again, I digress. I was dusting the windowsill, I had just watered the little cactus that I usually ignore, well, they sort themselves really don't they? They don't take much looking after. I heard Fred coming up the stairs, they are wooden. (it's an old building) Don't get me wrong, I can't hear Fred thumping up the stairs. Goodness, me no, he's quite light on his feet really. He'd make a good dancer. No, I hear him when he reaches the second flight. By then he has had enough of stair climbing, and he starts cursing, long and loud. That's what I hear.

As I was saying, he came up the stairs, and flung my office door open, shouting surprise as he did so. That wasn't a surprise. Remember, I'd heard him coming. He was on one knee, well, he was on two knees if I'm honest. I thought he'd fallen over, he hadn't, he was proposing. That's when I wet myself. He'd never shown any interest before now. Yet here he was, on his knees, waving a hazelnut latte and a crispy creme doughnut at me, and declaring undying love.

It's no wonder I wet myself. I stopped and thought for a few moments, for effect, and accepted his surprise proposal. I'm forty plus, I might not get another. I felt the need to ask why he had proposed with a drink and a doughnut. He said he hadn't, the drink and doughnut were because I had been his P.A. for five years. A celebration. The proposal had just coincided with the anniversary. That answered that question.

That was a few weeks ago, haven't had any surprises since, so haven't wet myself. Nothings changed, I still arrive late every day, Fred arrives later still. I did inform Brunhilda about Fred's proposal and, she has offered to make the vedding cake vith the icing. That's it really, I don't like surprises. Having said that, that one was not too bad. It could have been a lot worse. I have a friend who was once surprised by a .... I'm off again, aren't I?

I'll shut up now, I do like to go off on a tangent.

The Brooch

Cally Jenkins stood in front of the wall mounted, glass-fronted cabinet. The piece of jewellery that she had spotted when she was browsing the online auction list was simply stunning, standing here now, in the auction room, Cally could see that neither the brochure photograph or the online picture, had done it justice. Surrounded by equally attractive jewellery, the gold tone clown brooch just drew Cally in.

Cally wasn't a regular visitor to auctions, but, had been persuaded by her friend Gemma, who was moving into an old property, and she was looking for furnishings and decorative items to reflect the property's age. Having agreed to go, Cally decided to check the online list to see what was being auctioned. It was a general auction, mainly items from house clearances. Her friend informed Cally that this was a great way to buy, as prices were pretty reasonable, mostly if there were not too many people bidding. There was, rarely, if ever, a reserve price on items because usually, with house clearances, owners had died and families just wanted the items sold quickly.

'What on earth are you looking at?' Cally jumped at the sound of her friend's voice.

'Oh,' laughed Cally. 'I was in a world of my own, I think this brooch is gorgeous. I can't stop looking at it.'

'Ugh, that's freaky.' Said her friend, Gemma. 'You don't even like clowns, and that one is scary looking.'

'I know, that's the daft part,' said Cally. 'It isn't something I would generally be interested in, but I can't take my eyes off it.

Gemma shuddered. 'The eyes on that brooch are looking back at you too. You aren't going to bid on it are you?'

'Oh, I doubt I could afford it.' Replied Cally.

Cally sat down with Gemma at the back of the auction room. Both girls had numbered paddles to indicate if they were bidding on an item. While Cally had no plans to bid for anything significant, Gemma had seen a couple of small items of furniture she would definitely bid on if the price was right, and she was very keen to win the bidding on a large, blue and white porcelain washbowl on a stand. She could already picture it in her spare bedroom.

Cally was flicking through the brochure as the auction began. When she came to page two, the photo of the brooch, once more, caught her attention. Lot 57. Cally read the description. Gold-tone brooch. Clown head with coloured stones. Costume piece. Cally felt that the description didn't match what she was seeing. The brooch was indeed very golden in colour. The clown had an oval head and a slightly raised ' widow's peak' indicating that the clown had hair. The eye shapes were cut out, but a small, blue stone adorned the centre of the eyes. Just beneath each eye was a red tear-shaped stone, this gave the impression that the clown, though smiling, was, in fact crying. The smiling mouth also had a small lip shaped section cut out in its centre. The lower part of the brooch appeared to be the very wide lapels of a jacket and a neckerchief. The neckerchief was studded with red stones and looked like a polka dot scarf.

As she closed the brochure, Cally wondered why she was so drawn to the brooch. Gemma was right, she didn't like clowns, and it was rather creepy looking. How could something so creepy be that beautiful?

Gemma nudged Cally. 'This is it, this is the washbowl and stand I want. Wish me luck.' Cally waggled her thumb at Gemma and said, 'Good luck Gems.'

'Lot 49.' The auctioneer spoke into the microphone. 'Who will start the bidding at five pounds?' Gemma held her numbered paddle aloft and entered the bidding when the price reached eleven pounds. She finally secured the much-wanted item at fifteen pounds. She wasn't concerned that the bowl was chipped and had a hairline crack. It was going to hold Pot Pourri, not water. Her spare bedroom would not only look lovely, but it would also smell lovely too.

The next few lots were of no interest to either of the young women, and they sat quietly, just watching and listening as items were sold, or not. Eventually, it was Lot 57 that was brought to the attention of the bidding public. 'Shall we start the bidding at ten pounds?' Enquired the auctioneer. 'Surely it's worth that much to one of you lovely ladies!' 'No, ok, who will give me five to get started?' Still, no one showed any interest. Gemma turned to Cally and whispered quietly, 'I'm not surprised. Why would anyone want that scary thing?' The words were barely out of Gemma's mouth when Cally waved her numbered paddle in the air. The auctioneer's gavel banged down quickly, and Cally became the owner of the clown brooch for the princely sum of five pounds.

Gemma looked at Cally in amazement. Cally laughed at the look on Gemma's face and said, 'I'm not sure what happened then, my arm seemed to develop a life of its own. I certainly hadn't planned on buying the brooch, but at least the cost won't break the bank.' Gemma hadn't been lucky with her other bids, and both girls decided to pay for their items and go for a cuppa. Neither were interested in the remaining lots.

The two made their way outside into the High Street. Cally had dropped the brooch into her bag, and Gemma had arranged to have her washbowl and stand collected from the auction room later in the day. There was a small teashop across the road from the building they had just left, so they crossed over and went inside. Once comfortably seated, the waitress came over, and they ordered a pot of tea and toasted teacakes.

The two girls discussed their plans for the evening as they sat enjoying their refreshments. Gemma and her boyfriend would be stripping wallpaper from the lounge walls in Gemma's new house. Cally had a new book she was eager to get started. Reading and soft music. Cally's idea of a perfect evening.

As Cally and Gemma were leaving the teashop, an elderly lady reached out and grabbed Cally's wrist. She seemed to appear from nowhere. She thrust her face so close that Cally could feel the warmth of the old ladies breath, and smell the fetid aroma that emitted from her mouth as she spoke. 'Beware the funny man.' Cally stepped back in surprise and turned to look at Gemma who seemed equally surprised. Without feeling the woman release her wrist, Cally turned to look at her again. She had disappeared. 'What on earth was that about?' Asked Gemma, 'What did she say to you?' Cally told Gemma what the stranger had said. 'What could she have meant?' Queried Gemma. Cally shivered, feeling as though someone had just walked over her grave. 'Don't know Gems, she seemed a bit odd, not quite the ticket I'm thinking, and,' Cally pulled a face. 'She had terrible breath.'

Gemma laughed. 'Come on Cally, let's forget it and go home.

Once home, Cally entered her lounge. Unlike her friend, Cally opted for the minimalist look. There were few ornaments to be seen, and except for two paintings and an ebony wood framed mirror, the walls were bare, except for a coat of pale cream, matte emulsion. Cally sat down on the cream, soft Italian leather sofa. She always thought that this must be how it feels to sink into a fluffy cloud. She reached for her bag and took out the small brown leather box with its hook and eye fastener. This was the box she was given with the clown brooch tucked inside.

The box seemed quite old, much older than the brooch appeared to be. Early evening, Cally had eaten a chicken salad for supper. She opened a bottle of wine, put her CD player on low, and settled down on her fluffy cloud with the book she couldn't wait to get started.

Cally woke with a start, she had dozed off while reading her book. She smiled to herself and thought how a nice meal and two glasses of wine would do it every time. As she reached out to switch her table lamp on, movement caught Cally's eye, but what? Leaving the light off Cally looked at the walls in her lounge. With the light from the street-lamp outside casting shadows through her window, Cally was used to seeing them, but the shadows she saw now were moving, and they were on all of the walls. That was a little different to what she usually saw.

While Cally was wondering what was making the shadows, they disappeared. She shrugged her shoulders and presumed that a slight breeze had caught the curtains and caused the shadows to move. It was a few days later that Cally started to wonder if she was going mad.

Cally came in from work. It had been a busy day, and she was glad to be home. Thank goodness it was Friday. A whole weekend to relax. She went straight into the kitchen to put the kettle on to boil. A nice cup of tea was what she needed. As she entered the kitchen a stench wafted around her, it seemed familiar, but she wasn't sure why. Her first thought was the kitchen bin, but nothing, ever, got put in there that could smell so rotten. She gingerly opened the fridge door, half expecting to see rotting flesh sitting there, but at the same time, knowing she wouldn't.

As expected, the fridge was clean and fresh looking, all foodstuffs in their rightful place and on the right shelves. Cally closed the fridge door. As she turned, she thought she caught a glimpse of something, or someone, standing in the corner of the kitchen. Cally gasped, looked closer at the corner, and saw nothing. 'Beware the funny man.' Cally turned quickly, and sitting at the breakfast bar was the old lady who had grabbed her wrist in the teashop. 'Who are you?' Queried Cally, 'and how did you get into my flat? I'm going to phone the police.'

The old lady cackled. 'They can't help you, you have to help yourself. That brooch, get rid of it.'

'What do you mean?' Asked a very nervous Cally. There was no answer, the cackling crone had disappeared, taking with her the awful smell. Cally opened the fridge and removed a bottle of white wine, she reached for a glass and poured out a very generous measure. Taking a gulp of the wine, she wondered if she had just imagined what had happened. Surely she didn't imagine that malodorous stench or the old hag cackling in her kitchen, and how did she know about the brooch. One thing Cally was sure of, it had frightened her.

Gemma laughed. 'Cally, you are working too hard, you need to take a break. You are taking this far too seriously.' Cally had phoned her friend and told her what had happened. She hoped she would come and spend the evening with her, and maybe even stay the night. Instead, Gemma had laughed at her, and as good as suggested that she had imagined the whole thing. Cally asked Gemma how she could imagine the old lady being in her kitchen, hadn't she seen her too, when they were in the teashop. They couldn't both have imagined her that day, and, how could she possibly imagine a smell? Gemma told Cally she was sorry, she was busy this evening and couldn't come to the flat tonight. Cally was very disappointed, and more than a little upset. Hadn't they always been there for each other? Nothing ever prevented them from supporting one another in times of worry, stress or sadness. Till now.

After switching her phone off Cally went into the lounge and sank down into the soft leather sofa. Tucking her feet underneath her, she shuffled about until she was comfortable. Leaning on the arm of her seat, Cally rested her head in her hand. She had to sort herself out. Maybe Gemma was right, perhaps she did need a break from work, she had been swamped. Tears rolled, silently, down Cally's cheeks. What on earth is the matter with me, she wondered.

It was while Cally was sat quietly, reflecting on the conversation she'd had with Gemma that she noticed the shadows were back. As before, they were on all of the walls and moving. Cally sat transfixed, studying the dancing shadows. A tune popped into her head. The Circus Theme. Cally sat humming the tune to herself, and then, in a moment of clarity, realised what the shadows were......... But how?

She could see the trapeze swinging backwards and forwards. The high-wire springing up and down as someone edged their way across to the platform on the opposite side. The tumblers and acrobats and the clowns. They were all there. The Big Top was in her lounge, in shadow form, but there nevertheless.

Cally was awake, she wasn't dreaming, she certainly wasn't imagining what she was seeing. She was, however, still wondering how, and, why. Then there was The Circus Theme. A tune that had no reason to be in her head.

Cally had left the box containing the brooch in her handbag. She reached for her bag and, placing her hand inside, felt around for the small box. The box sat neatly in the palm of Cally's hand. She unhooked the fastener and opened the hinged lid. The clown brooch nestled neatly inside the box. 'Are you really the cause of my worries?' Cally spoke quietly, probably more to herself than the brooch. She removed the brooch from the box and stared at it. It's just a brooch, Cally thought to herself, just a simple brooch. 'Beware the funny man', the words that the old woman had said, not once, but twice. There are those who find clowns funny, even if I don't, thought Cally. How could she find out more?

There was a spookiness to the brooch amidst the beauty of it. Cally, although frightened by the happenings of the past few days, was also curious, she wanted to know more. But where should she start?

In bed that night, Cally slept fitfully, circus clowns filling her dreams. She rose early the following morning, determined to find out as much as she could about the brooch that was becoming the bane of her life. Over a breakfast of tea and toast, Cally decided to ring Gemma and see if she would help her. Surely she would, after all, if Cally hadn't gone to the auction with Gemma, she would never have seen, never mind bought, the wretched jewellery item.

'Hi Gemma, it's me, Cally, are you busy today?'

'I am if it's that damn brooch again,' answered Gemma.

'Gems, please listen,' Cally implored. 'I need to find out more about it, I wish you would help me.'

Gemma was quite adamant. 'No Cally, I won't. It's just a silly, ugly brooch that you have become obsessed about. If it bothers you so much, just throw it in the bin and forget about it.'

'I can't do that Gemma, I need to know more, if you don't help me, I'll do it by myself,' Cally could feel herself getting cross with Gemma, they never argued, so why now? The conversation ended on a bitter note, and both girls hung up.

Cally decided she couldn't worry about that now, she was going to see if she could find out where the brooch had come from. The gentleman in the auction room was very apologetic. 'I am so sorry, but we cannot give out private information. I am unable to say who brought the brooch in for auction.' Cally thanked him and left, trying to work out how she could get the information she wanted.

Once home, Cally decided to check out circus history on her laptop. Maybe it would offer up a few clues. She didn't need to. Within a few minutes of coming in Cally received yet another visitation. Though this time, not the odious old crone. Appearing from seemingly nowhere, a pretty young girl was standing in the centre of Cally's lounge. The sun was shining through the window, giving the lounge a bright and airy feel and it bathed the young girl in an eery glow. Unlike the old lady, who had frightened Cally, this visitor offered a feeling of calmness, and Cally heard herself saying hello, as though it were the most natural thing in the world for a person to manifest themselves in the middle of one's lounge.

'Hello.' The young girl spoke softly. 'Do you know why I'm here?'

'I'm hoping it's about the brooch I bought,' answered Cally. Then immediately told the girl about the problems it was causing, and specifically the tension between herself and her best friend.

The young girl nodded. 'That's what HE does best.'

'I don't understand,' said Cally. 'What do you mean, HE?' The young girl asked Cally to listen to her story.

Ava was born into a circus family. Her parents were high wire artists. They travelled the world over the years and performed their daring feats to vast and varied audiences, including royalty. She grew up knowing she too, would become a high wire walker and her parents encouraged her to practice on short, low wires almost from the time she could walk. By the time she was eighteen, there was nothing Ava couldn't do on the high wire. Her balance was perfect. Audiences loved her, she was the darling of the Big Top.

Ava's best friend was Olivia, or Ollie, as she called her. Ollie and Ava grew up together, and Ollie was destined to perform on the trapeze. It was all she ever wanted. Her parents were acrobats, but that wasn't for Ollie. For her, the trapeze offered thrills, excitement and glamour. Ava's parents were very strict, and this made Ava secretive. When she started walking out with Enrico, she told no one. Not even Ollie.

Whenever they could, Ava and Enrico would slip away from the circus site and go walking, hand in hand in the local park or by the river. Enrico told Ava how he would show her the sights in his beloved Spain. How they would marry and have children. Give up the circus life and keep orange groves instead. Ava believed him. So did Ollie. Neither girl knew that the other was in love with him, or that he had been cheating on both of them.

Enrico was a conceited young man who only loved himself. Underneath the clown make-up, he was handsome, and he knew it. When Ollie told Ava about her love for Enrico, they argued, each believing that they were the only one that he genuinely loved. In truth he loved neither, he just moved on to the next pretty girl who fell for his romantic chat.

Enrico had given Ollie a brooch, A brooch in his likeness. Such was his vanity. She cursed the brooch, as she cursed Ava. There was no forgiveness.

Ava told Cally that she and Ollie never made their peace. Enrico just left the broken-hearted girls and went to another circus. Ava, within days, missed her footing for the first time ever and plunged to her death. Ollie lived out her life with her only child, Sofia, Enrico and Ollie's illegitimate daughter. She remained bitter and unforgiving until her death.

Sofia was the person who took the brooch to the auction. She blamed the brooch and the father she never knew, for the miserable existence her mother had chosen. Cally could feel the tears streaming down her cheeks as she listened to Ava's story, but she was puzzled. She had two questions for Ava. When did this happen and if Ava was dead how did she know what followed after her death.

Ava smiled. 'It was 1958. Sixty years ago. We were eighteen years old and had the world at our feet. We allowed a man and a silly quarrel to ruin our friendship and our lives. Ollie never forgave me, but I couldn't move on without her. I still can't.'

'You have been with her all of the time.' Stated Cally.

'Yes.' Answered Ava. Then she disappeared.

Cally picked the phone up and dialled Gemma's number. The following morning Cally and Gemma stood on the stone bridge that crossed the fast flowing river. Cally opened the small box and let the brooch fall out and into the murky waters below. She then threw the box in. 'Good riddance.' Said Cally.

'Hear, hear.' Responded Gemma. As they walked away, Cally looked back. There were two people stood watching them. For a split second the old crone was stood with Ava, then, it was just Ava and Ollie. They smiled, and waved, and were gone. Cally knew they had made their peace and would spend eternity together.

Three months later, two young friends were sat dangling their feet in a meandering stream. Something gold glinted amongst the pebbles. One of the girls reached into the cool water and pulled out the shiny item. 'Oh, I love clowns.' She shouted gleefully.

Whitethorn

Whitethorn was a crescent-shaped road with houses on one side only. Opposite was an open green where daily, local kids played football, cricket and other games. Depending, of course, on the weather.

The road curved inward at the middle where the boy lived. From an upstairs window, and not without considerable difficulty, he could see both ends of the street. This never deterred the boy, he knew what he had to do. He went to bed at 8 00pm, not that the time mattered much, he wouldn't be sleeping for a long time. His bed was dirty, it always was, as were his pants and vest. He had already worn them for a week, even to school. Just one meagre blanket covered his bed and a few old coats. That didn't make up for the lack of heating in the room. Not many rooms had heating upstairs in the 1950s.

This particular bedroom was small and cramped with three beds in it. One for his parents, a bed for his 6-year-old sister and of course, a bed for his 9-year-old self. The boy would talk to his younger sister once they were in bed, but feigned sleep when his mother came to bed.

One rule of the house was, that whoever was last in always let themselves in by pulling the door key through the letterbox. The key was hung on a piece of string nailed to the inside of the door. The last one in would enter the house and retrieve the key by pulling it back through the letterbox. The string would then be wound around a nail above the letterbox to ensure no one else could use it.

The boy would lie in his bed and listen as his brothers and sisters came to bed. When they climbed the bare wooden stairs, he counted each brother and sister, one by one. It was 10 00pm. The house was now as quiet as it would ever be. There was only one person not home, and he was the reason the boy could not sleep.

His mother stirred in her sleep, but the boy knew it was time to rise. As quietly as he could, he rose from his bed desperately hoping he wouldn't disturb his sleeping mother and sister. He made his way to the landing at the top of the stairs. To his right was a window. He stood on tiptoes and stretched to view the light from the lamppost on the corner of the street. From the top of the wooden stairs, he could see the front door and the key still hanging below the letterbox. He positioned himself where no one would see him, and he waited. He waited for a full hour shaking from the cold and from fear.

At around 11-00pm a man appeared. Easily recognisable to the boy as he walked under the lamplight. The man stopped to light his cigarette, then turned towards the house. The boy had grown very adept at judging from the man's walk, what condition he was in. His gait was straight and steady. The boy returned to bed knowing that tonight at least, it would be a quiet night, and at last, he could sleep. His father was home and on this night, sober.

Hello Mum

The face stared at me from the open doorway. 'Hello, Mum.' Fourteen long years, and not one word from him, till now. This boy, to whom I gave life, and he gives me just two words. 'Hello, Mum.' What was I supposed to say to him? He wasn't even a boy now, he was a man. He'd be nearly thirty. I last saw him in 2003, I remember the date, why wouldn't I? It was three days before his fifteenth birthday.

It didn't make any sense, he just disappeared. His father and I searched for him, the police searched for him, his friends searched for him. Nothing. There were no clues, he wasn't seen on any CCTV cameras anywhere. He just disappeared into thin air. He was never found, and eventually, we were told to accept that our only child, who was so wanted, and so loved, was dead.

It was months before we slept properly if we ever really did again. We stopped going out, what if he came back, and we weren't here? What if he phoned, and no one answered? Our lives became a series of what ifs. Eventually, his friends stopped calling around, stopped asking after him. Our friends stopped inviting us out. It suited us both. We didn't want to be sociable, we had lost our boy, and their lives went on as usual.

Holidays, School Sports Day, School Prom, Exams, Exam results. Then later, University. Girlfriends. Marriage and Children. All taken from us when he disappeared. Now, he stands before me and says, 'Hello Mum,' like I only saw him yesterday.

As the years go by people assume all is well, life goes on, you have accepted your lot in life. This was your fate. How could they get that so wrong? You never accept, your life doesn't go on in the same way. How can it? We were told he must be dead, but there is a part of you that says no, he's out there... somewhere. He has to be.

When he first disappeared, we found ourselves going over, and over, and over, the days leading up to that fateful day. The day that changed our lives forever. Eventually, though, that stopped. It changed nothing. Four years to the day of his disappearance, his father took his own life. What would I say to my son if he returned?. His father didn't think about that when he did what he did.

Now, ten years on from that day, my son has returned. I have waited and longed for this moment for fourteen long, lonely years. 'Come on Mum. It's time to go, Dad's waiting.' I walk into my son's open arms, allowing myself a quick glance over my shoulder. I see myself lying in bed, the empty pill bottles, and a glass now devoid of its contents... Vodka. Yes, it's time to go.

The Wedding Gift

Today is my fortieth wedding anniversary. Ruby, I think, but I can't be sure. No matter, my wife died ten years ago. Was it a happy marriage? Who knows? We had been married for thirty years when she passed away. I think we became a habit, or maybe just comfortable, like a pair of shoes past their best. She hadn't been ill, she just didn't wake up one day.

The usual platitudes were thrown my way. 'Time heals', 'She didn't suffer', 'What a lovely way to go'. I got them all. The first few months passed by in a bit of a blur. I went through every day on autopilot. Time does indeed heal though, and every day became easier. I found a routine that worked for me.

Don't get me wrong, I missed my wife. She had cared for me well. Did we set the world alight? Not really. We had great holidays, no kids, and no family to speak of.

I had a mother. Strange woman. She loved me, I know that. But she had weird ideas. She's been gone a good few years now. I never knew my father. Not even sure if he's dead or alive. Given my age, sixty-eight next birthday, I presume he is probably dead, but I cannot be sure. Doesn't really matter, don't think he ever knew I existed anyway.

My late wife had a distant cousin, but I never met him, or her. Must have been one or the other. As I said, my mother was a strange woman.

This large glass jar is what she gave us for a wedding gift. It's full to the brim with stuff. Not sure what. I have never looked at it closely. It has lived in the same place, 'decorating' the mantlepiece for forty years, not once have I been tempted to remove the lid and examine the contents - until now that is. Today I am going to see exactly what my mother gave us.

I would never have believed you could fit so much into a jar that would probably hold about two pints of liquid. The lid unscrewed very easily, given the fact that it hadn't been removed in forty years. I thought age may have welded it to the jar. The contents are all on a tray. Not entirely sure quite what I will find amongst this melange. I thought emptying onto a tray was a pretty safe option, at least that way nothing could escape. It doesn't look inspiring. Colourful maybe, in parts. I can see a piece of string, three elastic bands, you know the ones I mean, the thick heavy ones that the posties keep the mail in bundles with. I am always picking them up off the front doorstep. There are several glass marbles in a variety of colours, numerous bits of paper.

For some reason, there are a couple of matchbooks, minus the matches, and a matchbox with a picture on the front, again, minus the matches. As I rummage through the contents on the tray, I am beginning to recognise a few things. My penknife. Always had that in my pocket as a kid. No self-respecting lad would be caught dead without a pocketknife. Mum bought it for me on my 8th birthday. I used to whittle bits of wood. Wow, I'd forgotten that. Nearly sixty years ago.

This blue and white marble, I won it off Georgie Bell, my best mate. I remember the day so well. It was the summer holidays, no school. We were always playing out in the street, football, cricket or tag. This day it was tag, and when I say I 'won' the marble, that isn't strictly true. To be honest, I wasn't a great marbles player. I lost all of my best marbles to Georgie, he was the marbles champ of our street. My big Tigers Eye marble, my Claydy and even my best Steely. Georgie won them all.

On this particular day though victory was mine. In my head anyway. The blue and white marble was Georgie's lucky marble. He won everything with that marble. I would have done anything to own it. Then my chance came. As we were running around the marble fell through a hole in Georgie's trouser pocket. It landed with a thud in the gutter. We both watched it roll, almost in slow motion, until it reached a drain and dropped in. We both dropped to our knees and peered down into the murky depths of the drain. The marble, much to our surprise, was perched precariously on a narrow ledge. It was unlikely that Georgie would be able to reach it if he could get his arm through the grid. He was short and dumpy, whereas I was more like a string bean.

As expected Georgie failed miserably. It was down to me to liberate the stricken marble, with Georgie informing me that, if I did so, the marble was mine. Nothing could have stopped me reaching through the grid into that mucky drain. I lay on my stomach in the gutter, my nose pressed up against the kerbstone, and I forced my arm through the grid almost to my armpit and retrieved the lucky marble. I dropped it in my pocket. I never played marbles with it, Georgie would have won it back easily. No, it was mine, and I wasn't parting with it.

I cannot believe I had forgotten about that. Georgie lives in Canada now, haven't seen him in the flesh for years, but I will remind him of that day next time we Skype.

What else is here? A couple of lead soldiers, a bus ticket. Oh! I do remember this tiny train engine. The Duke of Connaught. I recall a day at school, I must have been about 11 years old. The Headmaster was taking us for a lesson because our usual teacher was off sick. Mr Curzon was a decent sort, and he decided to veer away from our standard History project and tell us instead about how on May 9th 1904 the Duke of Connaught steam train made a record-breaking run from Bristol to Paddington in 99 minutes and 46 seconds. He made it sound so exciting. I remember telling my mother all about it, and, like every other boy in class that day, I was going to be a steam train driver and break speed records.

This Matchbox toy turned up in my Christmas stocking. I always carried it around in my trouser pocket, happy to show it off to anyone who was interested. I could have swapped it with friends for something else a hundred times, but nothing would have induced me to do that.

There are cigarette cards, a couple of old halfpennies and a threepenny bit. An old cinema stub is from Saturday Minors. Georgie and I never missed it. We always came out pretending to be Rocketman.

I kissed my first girl when I was at Minors. Betty Smethurst. Georgie wasn't impressed, he fancied her something rotten. Thinking back though, I think the next week she sat by Georgie and kissed him.

My first real girlfriend was when I was 17. We went out for a few months. Sylvia someone, her surname escapes me. She was a fashion-conscious girl. Long dark hair, mini skirts, knee length boots. The bus ticket is from when I took her to a Stones concert. It was 1967, who would have thought they would still be touring and performing in 2018.

Oh my word, this plastic ring is what I gave to Hilary when I asked her to marry me. It was Christmas Day 1975. I was 25 and Hilary was 23. I wanted the proposal to be a surprise but also wanted her to choose her own ring. It seemed to me that the ideal time to ask her was when the plastic ring fell from the Christmas cracker we had just pulled. Thankfully she said yes and immediately after Christmas when the shops reopened, we replaced the gaudy purple ring with a white gold solitaire engagement ring.

There are a myriad of small items on this tray, and the realisation has just hit me. They are the contents of my trouser pockets. My mother gave me a jarful of memories from my childhood, my youth and even my early manhood. She knew me well enough to know I would open it one day. I think in her strange way, she also knew that day would be after she was long gone. She may even have known that my wife would no longer be here either. I can only thank my mother now for giving me a gift more precious than gold, her love and my memories.

Hey, Can Anybody Hear Me?

The spotty youth was walking down the street. I say walking. I use the term loosely. Young men don't really walk do they? It's more a shuffle in my opinion, and those trousers. Don't get me started.

I had been watching him a while, headphones on his head (where else.. haha). I could hear the music as I watched, and tracked him, from my vantage point just above street level.

Did I actually say music? Hmm, debatable. Not content with scrambling his brain by failing to use the volume control, he was also trying to wreck his eyesight by texting on what looked like the smallest mobile phone in existence. He didn't look up once. He didn't actually notice that he had got dog poo on his left shoe.. correction, they don't wear shoes do they....trainer. He had dog poo on his left trainer.

'Hey, can anybody hear me?' I didn't shout the words, but I did wonder if he might hear me. He apparently didn't so I tried again. 'Hey, can anybody hear me?' Nothing... oh well, I tried. He just walked under an articulated lorry, oops. Oh, just before I go, let me introduce myself. Lucifer's the name, or Black Angel, or Satan may be more familiar to you. No matter. My job is to ensure that heaven and hell get its full quota every day. As you can see reader, I do take my job very seriously. Ta ta - for now, anyway.

The Watering Hole

The sun is just rising, creeping up and glinting through the Acacia trees like a big, orange, ball. The noise is like no other, Africa has its own incredible sound. It is the sound of the African bush waking up to another scorching, hot, day. The early birdsong just adds to a cacophony of noise. The distant trumpeting of an elephant, the faraway roar of a big cat, the braying zebra, the barking of the wild African dogs and the snuffling of the warthogs, but it is the ever-present, overriding, chirruping sound of the cicadas, and other insects, that really determines Africa's individual soundtrack.

Herbie, the very friendly, but nosy heron, is wading through the water in the large waterhole that is just off the centre of the animal reserve. He's looking for breakfast. Any time now his head will dip down into the still water and he will catch himself a tasty fish or two. Because he is so nosy, he knows everybody and everything. He doesn't miss much.

I am going to leave you in his competent hands. OK, wings then. He will make an excellent tour guide. On this very unique tour though, there is one noticeable difference. The sights come to you. Please sit back and enjoy the delights of this entertaining watering hole. Oh yes, just one other thing. Herbie doesn't know he's your tour guide, so don't make a sound. Just listen, and you will hear all about life in the African bush as seen through the eyes of its occupants.

'Morning Herbie,' said a very tired looking elephant.'

Morning Mrs Ellie, how are the offspring this fine morning?' Asked Herbie.

'Naughty as ever Herbie,' sighed Mrs Ellie, 'I am at my wit's end. Twins are such hard work. Yesterday they both got their heads caught in an Acacia tree. Took three of us to get them out.'

'Eddy, Ernie, say good morning to Mr Herbie, wave your

trunks at him please.' Mrs Ellie requested.

'Morning Eddy, morning Ernie.' Said Herbie. The two young elephants were squirting water at each other and took no notice of their mother or Herbie. Herbie laughed. 'Far too busy for good mornings Mrs Ellie, I don't envy you, it's a good job you have your mother and sisters to help you keep them in line.'

Curly Croc is lying close to the water's edge. 'Hello, Herbie my mate.' Curly grinned at Herbie slyly. 'How are you doing?'

Herbie glanced nervously at the crocodile. 'Oh, hello Curly didn't see you lurking there. 'I'm very well thank you, just come out for breakfast, have you eaten?'

Curly smiled his sly smile again. 'I have, it was a delicious breakfast this morning. A few fish, a couple of toads, two rats and a porcupine.' Herbie visibly relaxed knowing Curly wasn't hungry right now, and would happily lie on the dry, sandy bank sunning himself. As Herbie waded past, Curly winked, 'See you later Herbie.'

Herbie smiled and muttered to himself, 'Not if I see you first.'

Moving through the water Herbie sees Jerry and Diana Goose with their offspring, all eight of them, gliding on the surface of the large pond. 'Keep them close Jerry,' warned Herbie. Curly is near the reeds, he says he's eaten, but you can't be too careful when he's around. You know how sneaky he can be.' '

Thanks for the warning Herbie,' said Jerry. 'Come on now, all bunch together, Mr Croc is on the bank, we don't want any mishaps.'

Herbie spots a couple of his friends on the far side of the watering hole and flies over to greet them. Flying is much quicker than wading. He comes in to land by two large balls of animal dung. 'Hello Herbie,' said a quiet voice, coming from somewhere by his feet.

'Hello Delia, how are things?' Asked Herbie, looking down

towards the ground.

'Oh you know, very busy as usual. This animal dung won't spread itself, or break down without our help.'

'No Delia, it won't. You, Danny and the teamwork awfully hard.' Herbie agreed. 'You do a sterling job, if it weren't for you Dung Beetles, it would be everywhere. Just think of the flies.'

At the mention of his name, Danny said, 'Can't stop to chat Herbie, if we don't find soft ground for the dung to sink into nothing will grow next year, and there will be no vegetation, and none of us will have any food. We have to return this dung back to the earth, after all, that's where it started.' Delia and Danny then lifted up their back legs placed them on the dung heaps and started walking backwards, like circus acrobats, pushing the dung along. 'Bye Herbie,' the pair shouted.

'A dung beetles work is never done.' Herbie chuckled, ' bye you two.'

Herbie looks up at the sky, the sun's quite high. Time is moving along.

'Hey Herbie, how you doing?'

'Hello, Sylvia, not seen you around in a while.' Answered Herbie.

'No, I have been on the plains with my family.' Sylvia replied. 'I am trying to teach my youngsters how to catch a snake. No good being a Secretary bird and not be able to catch a snake.'

'Well no,' agreed Herbie, 'Be like one of mine not catching fish. Can they get it?'

She shouted, 'No, they can't. They will not stamp their feet on the snake, so the wretched things get away. They can get toads and insects, no problems there, but a snake, not a chance. Oh well, must persevere with them,' she laughed. 'Haven't raised a brood yet that couldn't learn.'

' Yoo-hoo, Herbie,' over here, in the reeds.'

'What do you want Curly?' Asked Herbie. 'I have better

things to do than fall for your silly tricks. You stay out of my way, and I will stay out of yours.'

'That's not very friendly Herbie Heron,' said the disgruntled Crocodile.

'I've known you too long Curly. I don't trust you or your family, you are all a bunch of rogues and villains.' Curly slithered down into the water. Herbie took flight and flew to a nearby solid looking branch. He perched there with a good view of the water. He kept one eye on Curly as he moved stealthily across the watering hole.

'Not seen much of the Springbok or Kudu families today Mrs Ellie,' shouted Herbie from his high perch.

'No, you won't have,' Mrs Ellie shouted back at Herbie. ' Lavinia Lioness and her cubs moved into the area yesterday. The Springboks and Kudus are keeping a very low profile.' 'Ah, I don't blame them.' Replied Herbie.

'Oh, here's Gloria and Geoffrey coming,' announced Mrs Ellie. 'I can't hang around here watching them, I shall be a nervous wreck after what happened last time.'

'Eddy, Ernie, I will not tell you two again, get that mud washed off yourselves now. It's time to go.' The twin elephants hosed each other down. 'Bye Herbie, see you tomorrow.'

'Bye Mrs Ellie.' Answered Herbie, as he watched the three elephants trundle into the bush towards home.

Two giraffes strolled past the tree that Herbie was perched in. 'Not often we get to chat eye to eye with you Herbie,' stated Gloria, and pulled a few leaves to chew on, from the branch where Herbie was perching.

'No,' answered Herbie. 'I do prefer my feet in the cool water when it's so hot, but I'm keeping my eye on Curly Croc. I have a better view up here, I suspect he's up to no good as usual.'

Geoffrey added his bit. 'He's a shifty character.'

'He is Geoffrey.' Agreed Herbie.

'I thought I heard Mrs Ellie. Did I imagine it, Herbie?' Asked Gloria, slightly puzzled.

'Haha, no Gloria, you didn't imagine it. She was here with the twins, but once she saw you and Geoffrey coming, she rushed off.'

'Oh!' Exclaimed Gloria. 'Should I be offended?'.

'Goodness me no,' stated Herbie. 'It's just that she hasn't got over the shock yet, of seeing Geoffrey lose his footing and slip down onto his knees in the mud last week. The sight of two game wardens, a hoist, and a Land Rover, being needed to get him back on his feet was all too much for her nerves.'

'I know how she feels, it didn't thrill me much either.' Gloria answered a little indignantly.

'It wasn't a lot of fun for me either,' retorted Geoffrey. 'It was very embarrassing. I was mortified when I couldn't get myself up.

'Well, you certainly worried Mrs Ellie, Geoffrey.' Said Herbie.

The two giraffes ambled off to the water's edge. Herbie sat very still, almost holding his breath as Geoffrey splayed his front legs and fidgeted himself into a comfortable position for drinking.

'Oh do be careful Geoffrey,' implored Gloria. 'We really DON'T want a repeat of last weeks fiasco.'

'Is this the first time you have been back since Geoffrey's mishap Gloria?' Enquired Herbie.

'It is Herbie,' replied Gloria. 'It's taken him a few days to feel like walking this far. We stayed close to home for a while, but couldn't stay away forever.'

'WATCH OUT HERBIE.' Before Herbie was able to watch anything, there was a flurry of feathers and a thud, as a rather large something landed next to him. Herbie steadied himself as the unexpected visitor nearly bounced him off his perch.

'Hello Herbie,' said a rather doleful voice. Herbie turned his head to the left and looked at the very miserable figure of Vic the Lappet-faced Vulture. 'Oh it's you Vic.' Said a ruffled Herbie. 'I do wish you would land a bit gentler.'

'Sorry,' said Vic. 'I was looking out for a carcass, couldn't see one, and I didn't notice the tree. Came in a bit fast.' Vic shook his bald head and turned his head from side to side. 'Think I have done myself a mischief.' Stated the morose bird in a very monotone voice.

'Honestly Vic, I am surprised you are let out alone. Now, what have you done?' Herbie looked at Vic in disbelief.

'It's my neck,' said Vic, turning it from side to side again. Think I have damaged it.' Herbie agreed and said, 'it does look a bit bent'.

'It's always bent,' replied Vic. 'We weren't all blessed with willowy necks and long legs you know. Some of us drew the short straw.'

Herbie was about to reply, but luckily Gloria and Geoffrey passed by on their way home and possibly stopped a falling out between the feathered friends.

'Hello, Vic. Unusual to see you out and about without the others.' Gloria knew that the vultures usually travelled together.

'How are Vinny, Veronica, Valda and.. that one whose name always escapes me, he has to be different,' said Gloria.

'Oh you mean Reynard.. he's always been a bit of an oddball. His name is really Valentine you know, but he insists on being called Reynard. Everyone is well thank you Gloria, and nice to see you up on your legs again Geoffrey.' Vic then added that he had to be off now, and flew off almost as quickly as he had arrived.

'Do you think he could get more miserable?' Herbie asked the two giraffes. They all laughed and said their goodbyes. Herbie flew back down to the water, the sun would be setting soon.

'Still here, Herbie?' Curly smiled at him.

'Just thinking about going Curly, why are you still hanging around?' Enquired Herbie.

'Oh, you know me, Herbie, always first in the pool and last out.'

'Cooey, Herbie.'

'Hello Zinnia, you are very late today.' Herbie shouted across to the far side of the pond where Zinnia Zebra and her sister Zandra were standing.

'I know Herbie, we normally wander down with Gloria and Geoffrey, but Zac went missing, and Mummy had an attack of the vapours.'

'Ah, you were the search party were you!' Shouted Herbie. 'Where was he this time?'

'Down by the hippo pool again with Hector and Harriet Hippo and Kirsty that flighty Kudu. They will all end up in trouble if they aren't careful.'

'Oh dear,' said Herbie, as he waded across the pond, leaving Curly to his own company. 'He never learns, does he. Well, we don't need gang culture. We have enough to put up with the Hyena family and that pack of wild dogs that moved into the area. We don't need homegrown thugs in the mix.'

'Never fear Herbie, Mummy and Daddy have had words with Zac, he's only allowed to go out with them now. He's banned from mixing with the Hippos, and he can only see Kirsty when she is with her brothers. Kevin and Kirk will keep a very close eye on them.' Commented Zandra, rather sharply, making sure that Herbie knew the Zebras kept their family under control. She wasn't having him casting aspersions.

Herbie knew it was time to go. 'Best be off now,' he announced. 'See what kind of day my Hannah has had. She went out with her friends for lunch, trying that new pond that everyone is talking about. Might give it a go myself tomorrow. A change is as good as a rest they say.' As he flew off, he shouted down, 'Don't hang around now girls. It will be dark soon, and Lavinia Lioness is back with her cubs.. stay safe.'

That was just one day in the life of an African watering hole. It happens every day, at every watering hole, river and pond across the African Continent. I hope you enjoyed this little glimpse.

The Image

'The colours are dull thought the viewer. She peered closely at the painting hanging on the gallery wall. 'Yes,' she thought, 'definitely dull.' She moved along to look at something more colourful. A young couple, holding hands and more intent on looking at each other, stopped in front of the painting. 'Ooh, that's boring' commented the young woman.

Her art student boyfriend, laughed, and said, 'You can't say that about a famous painting.' They wandered off towards the exit. The elderly gentleman sat down on the hard wooden seat positioned in front of the painting. He rummaged around in his rucksack and pulled out a small, plastic box. After placing his bag on the floor, he proceeded to remove the lid from the box. He took out a ham roll, and as he studied the painting, he took a bite out of his roll. 'Hmm,' he thought. 'Nice bit of ham this.' He was so engrossed in his ham roll, and in studying the painting, that he didn't notice the middle-aged, uniformed man, walking towards him.

'Excuse me, sir,' said the man, 'I'm afraid we don't allow eating in the gallery.'

'Oh, no matter,' said the elderly gentleman. 'I have finished now,' and he popped the last of the ham roll into his mouth. He picked up his rucksack and dropped the plastic box inside. As he walked away from the painting, he cast a last look at it over his shoulder. Shaking his head, he thought to himself, 'and they call that art.'

'What a marvellous subject Darling.' The well dressed and very well spoken woman addressed her husband.

'A touch of Yellow Ochre used there my sweet, and maybe a hint of Ultramarine.' They stood together examining the painting, each thinking how much more they understood the art world since they had joined the village painting class two weeks ago. They studied their brochure and headed off arm in arm to go and critique another painting.

A small family group shuffled in front of the painting. The young boy pushed his older sister. It was evident that this wasn't his thing at all, and he didn't want to be there. 'Mum, tell him, he keeps shoving me.' The girl was seventeen and about to start Art College. Mum and Dad were being supportive and showing an interest, hence the family visit to the gallery. The young boy was lying on his stomach across the bench, his arms stretched out. He was pretending to be an aeroplane. 'Stop that,' said his Dad in a loud whisper. 'Why can't you look at the picture?'

'It's a Van Gogh painting for goodness sake.' The seventeen years old stated, with some indignance.

The boy answered with 'Who is he then?' And why is his first name Van?'

'His first name was Vincent, his name was Vincent Van Gogh,' explained Mum.

'You said was, is he dead? What did he die of?' The boy asked.

'I don't know,' Mum answered. She was getting irritated now. 'I do know he cut his ear off though.'

Her son was now very interested. 'Why did he cut his ear off? Is that why he died?'

'No son, that's not why he died, but he wasn't well when he cut his ear off.' Mum wished she had never started this conversation. 'Just look at the lovely painting,' Mum said.

'Lovely painting?' Said the boy in disbelief. 'Its A Pair Of Shoes.'

One Day

The old man wandered along the street with his head down. It was a hot, sultry day and thunder was forecast. The old man seemed to be looking for something; his head moved from left to right as his eyes scanned the pavement. Every now and then he would bend down quickly. He seemed very agile for a man of advancing years. Whatever he picked up he slipped into the pocket of his light coloured jacket. A jacket that had seen better days.

He heard the first rumble of thunder in the distance and made the decision to head home before the rain started. Home was a small, dilapidated, two bedroom cottage situated at the end of a rather smart avenue. The old man wasn't the most popular neighbour in the avenue. His very overgrown garden and its contents really didn't match the other pristine gardens with their bowling green lawns and neatly trimmed shrubs. The residents of Berkley Avenue had tried many times to have the old man removed from their neighbourhood, but with no level of success.

The old man reached the avenue just as the first spots of rain fell. He hurriedly made his way to the far end where his cottage was. He pushed open the broken gate and entered his garden. Amongst the weeds and brambles were old car tyres and broken garden pots. Propped up against the old, gnarled apple tree was an exhaust pipe. There were numerous car parts dotted about in varying states of decay. The old man would find a use for them though. One day.

He removed the door key from his trouser pocket and unlocked the front door. Pushing the door open took considerable strength, as it only opened a few inches. The old man squeezed inside.

To the untrained eye, what greeted the old man in the hallway was rubbish, junk and lots of it. Newspapers, in several piles, were stacked against one wall. Several bin-bags, tied and placed in a corner, threatened to spill over into the narrow walkway that had been forged from the front door to the lounge door. There were two dolls prams and three Christmas trees. One very highly decorated, and giving an air of festivity to the messy, cluttered hallway. But to the trained eye of the old man, he would find a use for all of this stuff. One day.

He entered his lounge to more of the same. Bin bags of goodness knows what, children's toys, (mostly broken), and furniture. There were two small coffee tables, a pair of curtains artistically draped over the back of an armchair with the stuffing coming out of the seat. Kitchen chairs, dining chairs and a variety of shelving.

The old man reached into his jacket pocket and pulled out the contents. A small piece of string, a glass marble with a blue flash at its centre, a pink bottle top and the arm from a little plastic doll. He placed his treasures on top of a battered, tin drum with a broken strap.

As the thunder rumbled above him, the old man smiled to himself. He knew he was a hoarder, but he would find a use for all of this stuff. One day.

The Little Christmas Tree

It was the early 1950s, and the forest was lit up. Fairy lights shone all around making the snow covered trees twinkle like a million stars in the night sky. It was December, nearly Christmas, and time for the Christmas trees to be dug up and potted ready for the people to come and buy them.

The Christmas trees weren't too keen on being uprooted from their home in the forest, they liked the snow around their feet in the winter, and the sun filtering through their branches in the summer. For one little tree, in particular, it was terrifying. He was only young, barely five years old and quite small. He was in the nursery section of the forest and the smallest of all the young trees. He was trembling, he knew that soon he could be whisked away to anywhere.

He had heard the other trees talking, and he didn't want to leave the only home he had ever known. All too soon the noise of excited little voices reverberated around the forest, and the trees could feel the vibrations in their roots from all of the feet trampling the very ground they lived in.

One small boy had wandered away from the busy part of the forest and was very close to the nursery. 'Oh' said the little tree when he saw the small child. The little tree was very frightened. The small boy walked over to the little tree and looked at him. They were about the same height. 'Oh,' the little tree said again. The small boy's eyes opened very wide, and in disbelief asked the little tree, 'did you just say oh'?

'You heard me' exclaimed the little tree.

'I did' said the small boy, 'and I didn't even know trees could talk, especially tiny ones like you'.

'Don't be so rude' said the little tree. 'You're no bigger than me, and you talk.'

'Why did you say Oh?' Asked the small boy.

'Because I'm scared to leave my home' explained the little tree. 'I can't live in a pot, there won't be any room for my roots to spread, I will never grow big and strong.' The little tree quivered and shook so much that the snow covering his branches fell off and landed in a heap at the base of his short trunk.

'Oh dear' said the small boy, 'Do you think I could help you?'

'How?' asked the little tree sadly.

'Don't know yet, I shall have to think,' stated the small boy, almost to himself.

'Joey, Joey, where are you?' A man was calling out, and the small boy answered.

'I'm here Daddy.'

'Thought I'd lost you,' said the man 'What would Mummy say if I went home without you?' Come on now, the Christmas tree is on the trailer, it's time to go.'

'Daddy wait,' said the small boy, 'Can I have my own Christmas tree to grow in the garden? Please Daddy, please,' begged the small boy. The man thought for a moment, then said, 'Well, I don't suppose it will hurt, it will teach you how to care for a living, growing tree. Shall we look around for a nice one?'

'No Daddy, I have already chosen this one' said Joey, pointing to the little tree.

'Hmmm,' said Daddy, 'That's very little.'

'It's the one I'd like please'. The small boy looked at his Daddy and smiled.

'OK' said Daddy let's talk to the tree seller.' The small boy winked at the little tree.

The little tree was soon carefully dug up from his nursery bed and replanted in a temporary pot. All of this was done under the watchful eye of the little boy. Once home the small boy wasn't interested in decorating the big Christmas tree, he was more concerned that his little tree got planted as soon as possible so that his roots could spread out and he could start to grow.

Over the years the little tree and the small boy grew big and strong together. The small boy tended his tree with loving care and always chatted to him, but strangely the little tree never spoke to him ever again.

Christmas was their special time, and the growing boy never failed to visit the now very big tree on Christmas Eve when he would remind the tree how they found each other. Christmas 2016 arrived, and the Christmas tree had stood tall and proud in the boys garden for over sixty years. But where was his friend on this Christmas Eve? He always found a few moments to come and chat with him at this time of year. Quietly, almost shyly, a small child came and stood at the base of the very tall tree. He was all wrapped up in a warm hat, coat and scarf, and he had his welly boots on. 'Hello great big tree' said the small child. 'Grandpa asked me to come.'

'Who?' Asked the big tree.

'My Grandpa told me how he brought you home to live in his garden when he was little like me' said the small boy.

'Well, where is he?' Asked the big tree. '

He went to live with the angels,' the boy answered, and a big, fat, wet, tear rolled down his chubby cheek.

'Oh' said the big tree sadly.

'You do talk then' said the small child. 'Grandpa said you did, but I didn't really believe him.' The small child also added, 'Grandpa said that if he could join us, he would.'

'I only talk when I need to,' said the big tree.'Will you visit me like he did?'

'Yes, I promised my Grandpa that I would.' Just at that moment a shooting star flew across the sky and started to fall to earth. It didn't reach the ground though, it landed on top of the great big Christmas tree. The small boy looked up to the top of the tree and smiled, the shooting star twinkled back at him. 'Grandpa,' whispered the small boy. The big, tall, tree sighed. 'Oh'.

So on this Christmas Eve a small boy, his Grandpa and his Grandpas tree were together. The snowflakes were fluttering around them, and they knew that they would spend many more Christmases together. The tree would grow bigger and taller still. The small boy would also grow big and strong, and Grandpa would watch over them both, just as he always had.

Romany Girl

Sitting on a log, fourteen-year-old Rosie Perkins gazed around her. She was drinking in the surrounding woodland. Sniffing the air like a vixen seeking her pups. Rosie didn't go to school. This was her school, the great outdoors, and she loved it.

Surrounded by nature, Rosie's classrooms were the open fields, the hills and dales and the riverbanks, anywhere in fact where she could sit and just watch, and listen, and smell the countryside. Rosie could write a little, her mum had taught her the basics, she could read a little too. Enough to get by. Rosie could also draw, and no one had taught her that. She just could.

Home for Rosie was a very gaily painted, horse-drawn caravan with an arched roof. The only home she had ever known, and where she lived with her mum, dad and grandmother. The horse that pulled the caravan was a Gypsy Cob, and piebald in colour, with feathered heels. His name was Spirit, and it was Rosie's job to look after him.

Rosie loved Spirit, and she cared for him most diligently. After her dad unharnessed him from their caravan at the end of each travelling day, Rosie would feed and water the horse and brush him till he shone. He was indeed a handsome horse.

Rosie was only eight years old when her dad bought Spirit from the Appleby Horse Fair. She remembered the time so clearly. They went every year in June, but that year was special because she was getting her very own horse. She knew he was to be a working horse, but he was still going to be hers, and she was the one who would care for him. She called him Spirit because she had heard her dad telling someone that the horse had spirit. She wasn't sure what it meant, but she liked it.

Appleby Horse Fair was always a fun place to be. Meeting up with friends and family, the music, the stalls, other colourful caravans and the Sands, the shoreline of the River Eden in the centre of Appleby where the boys rode their horses, bareback, into the river enabling the horses to be cleaned. Days before the fair started was a time of preparation. A busy time for Rosie, her mum and her grandmother. First, there was the heather to be picked from the moors. Rosie loved this, out in the fresh air amongst the gorse and ferns, the wind blowing through her long, raven coloured hair. Once picked, it was the job of her grandmother to sort out the best sprigs and bind the stems with white ribbon, this made the heather easier to sell when it looked so pretty.

Then there were Rosie's sketches. Small pencil sketches of landmarks she had seen In towns, they had passed through while travelling. These were always much sought after, as were her watercolours. The wildflowers she loved so much were captured in great detail. The pastel yellow primroses of Springtime, the crimson field poppies of Summer, and the bright, sunshine yellow kingcups thriving in the boggy marshes. All these and more were offered for sale in the towns and villages as they ambled their way to the Horse Fair.

Rosie's mum would tell fortunes, her crystal ball always close at hand. One day Rosie would do the same, but not yet. Her dad sat at the front of the caravan, steering Spirit in the right direction.

Rosie's grandmother sat by his side in good weather, while Rosie and her mum chose to walk the country lanes foraging as they went. Rosie's classroom changed with the seasons. In Spring she would sit by streams and ponds, fascinated by the frogspawn and the changes that took place. Watching in wonder at the small, wriggling tadpoles as they emerged from the spawn. Later, of course, their transformation into frogs, no bigger than her thumbnail. The birds collecting materials to build their nests and the trees bursting into blossom and bringing colour to the landscape.

When Summer arrived Rosie's skin would turn nut brown from the suns rays, and she would spend her days picking field mushrooms which her dad would cook on the open fire that was lit every evening. She'd sit sketching, as she dangled her feet in meandering streams, or she quietly watched as rainbow trout swam in and out of the reeds.

As Autumn approached, the days were shorter and a little colder. But that brought fresh delights. Rosie would pick the blackberries that grew in the hedgerows, always irresistible. She would have to eat some of the dark, juicy, fruits which always left telltale purple stains on her fingers and lips. As the leaves on the trees changed from green to the rich, russets and gold colours of autumn, Rosie would collect the shiny conkers from the base of the sprawling Horse Chestnut trees.

Finally, winter would arrive, and Rosie travelled in the caravan with her mum and grandmother. Her dad, as always, happy to be steering Spirit towards their next destination. Where would their travels take them? Maybe to Ireland where Rosie loved to sketch the white painted cottages. This is where her maternal grandparents lived, though their travelling was only in their homeland now. Rosie always enjoyed her visits there.

Or perhaps Wales would be next where mountains and hillsides created new classrooms and playgrounds for Rosie. Where the Winberries grew in great abundance in late summer. Wherever Rosie and her family travelled to, Rosie knew that life for her was extraordinary, and she wouldn't swap it for anything.

It had been a hard couple of years for Rosie Perkins and her family. Now, aged almost sixteen, Rosie and her parents had travelled to Ireland to visit her maternal grandparents. They had been unable to bring their own travelling home with them, so their beautiful gypsy caravan and Rosie's horse Spirit had been left in the care of friends.

While Rosie's early years had been idyllic, the last couple had been hard. Jobs, difficult to come by, made money scarce. This, coupled with a harsh winter, took its toll, it saw them all struck down with influenza. This bout of sickness had claimed the life of her paternal grandmother, and Rosie had been left saddened at the loss of, not only a grandmother, but also a teacher, a friend, and, a travelling companion.

It was early Spring, and the air was cold and damp, the mist hung low over the land, and it swirled around the feet and ankles of farm workers in the fields. Rosie and her mother huddled close together for extra warmth pulling their shawls tightly around their heads and shoulders. They were sat in the donkey cart that Rosie's father had bought on arrival in Ireland. It didn't offer the same warmth and protection from the elements that their covered caravan did. But it was transport, and they had a long way to go.

Mary and Patrick McDonagh (Rosie's maternal grandparents) were Irish travellers, but age had convinced them to settle and to ease out of their travelling life. They were now living in Dundalk. Dun Dealgan to give it its Irish name, meaning Dalgans Fort.

Dundalk, County Louth is close to the border of Northern Ireland, where Mary and Patrick spent some of their early married life travelling. Roughly halfway between Dublin and Belfast, it was close enough for them to travel to the North in a warmer summer, to visit friends and family still living there. They could never be completely free of their Nomadic lifestyle.

Not just the ease in which The McDonaghs could travel to the North helped them to decide on settlement in Dundalk. It is sheltered by the Cooley and Mourne Mountains to the North. To the West and South, undulating hills. These gifts of nature offer protection, and while winters could be cold, summers were mild. Not quite such inclement weather as in other parts of the country.

Home now was a traditional Irish cottage, with whitewashed walls and a thatched roof. It nestled in the Dundalk countryside where the Castletown River flowed gently down to Dundalk Bay.

The mist had finally cleared, and the sun broke through bringing some much-needed warmth to the bones of the weary travellers. They had nearly reached their destination. The donkey clip-clopped his way down country lanes pulling his heavy burden. Jake, the donkey, would be glad to see his journey over too.

Rosie could see her grandparent's white-walled cottage in the distance, glowing like a beacon in the spring sunlight. Rosie's father veered off the country lane, and the donkey cart bumped its way along a very rough track. Rosie jumped from the donkey cart, opened the creaky, old, wooden gate and her father steered the cart through. The dusty track would lead them to the door of the cottage.

Rosie opted to walk the rest of the way, she wanted to take in the sights and sound of the place she would call home for a while. As she ambled along the track, she watched the donkey cart bouncing along the rutted track in front of her. Being early spring the trees were just coming into leaf, blossoms were bursting forth, and the birds were gathering materials for their nest building.

The Dundalk countryside was busy. Standing quietly for a few moments, Rosie listened. The birds were singing, and she smiled. This would be a new adventure for her. She could hear the Castletown River flowing fairly close by, maybe she could go fishing with Granda? Realising she couldn't see the donkey cart, she lifted her heavy skirt and hopped, skipped, and ran, along the rough track to try and catch up with her parents. It didn't take her long.

Rosie's grandparents were waiting on the doorstep with arms open wide. As the donkey cart was drawing to a halt, Rosie raced past it straight into the arms of her Nana. Granda stood by smiling. They were all ushered into the small cottage by Nana, while Granda took the now free of burden Jake, and led him to a patch of grass so that he could graze.

The inside of the cottage was dark. The small window it boasted didn't let in a great deal of light. The floor was dry and dusty from the compacted clay and mud. A fire was burning inside a roughly built hearth. This is where Nana did her cooking. She had a large cauldron shaped pot resting on a trivet. The pot was filled with a rich, bubbling stew. There wasn't much meat in there, but there were plenty of vegetables, and it would be tasty and nourishing. She had been given a freshly baked loaf which would be used to mop up the flavoursome gravy.

Soon the family were seated around the small kitchen table. It was a bit of a squeeze, but they managed. The travellers were hungry after their journey and tucked into their meal with relish. Rosie and her parents had been staying with Nana and Granda about a week, and Rosie had already been out fishing with Granda twice. They hadn't caught anything, and they were teased mercilessly by Rosie's dad. As Rosie petted Jake the donkey, she thought back over her first week. She enjoyed the fishing with Granda, and she had fun learning how to make good, wholesome food on the open hearth fire with Nana. But by far, the best times were when they all sat around the brightly burning fire, and Nana told them stories of how the Irish travellers lived when she was only Rosie's age.

Nana told how when she and Granda were first married in Northern Ireland, they had nothing. No donkey cart to travel in, and no tarpaulin to make a bender tent for shelter. Rosie asked what a bender tent was, and Granda explained that it was a shelter made by using flexible branches of hazel or willow. These were often referred to as withies. The withies would be lodged into the ground, bent, and woven together to form a dome shape. Granda told the interested Rosie how sturdy the bender tents were and, when a tarpaulin was thrown over the domed withies and weighted down well, what beautiful shelters they made. They would hold steady in high winds, and could even be heated during the cold winters, using a wood-burning stove.

It would be many a long day before they had a bender tent. In the meantime they would walk miles each day, hoping for fieldwork. Nana said that if they were lucky, the farmer would let them sleep in the barn and give them bread and cheese for their hungry bellies. A not so generous farmer would see them go hungry, would throw a few measly pennies their way for a job done, and the night would be spent sleeping under a hedge, snuggled together to try and keep warm.

In towns and villages, Nana told Rosie she would spend pennies in the small shops, buying combs, needles, coloured threads and scissors. These items she would sell to ladies in the big houses, out in the countryside where there were no shops. She always charged a little more than she had paid. Sometimes they would pay her with a small food parcel. Tea and sugar were gratefully received. If Nana and Granda were really lucky, they could be offered work for a few weeks. Granda would clean the big house chimneys and mend the pots and pans. Nana would work in the kitchens as a scullery maid It was hard work for little reward, but they ate well.

Nana learned to bake bread and churn butter and Rosie's mouth watered when Nana told her how there was nothing nicer than bread, eaten, warm from the oven, and buttered with the butter you churned yourself. But, they were travellers, or Tinkers, as some called them. They always moved on.

They travelled the North, and Nana explained they were hard

but happy times. The people were good and kind. Ladies having their fortunes told would give potatoes and cabbages, which Nana cooked for a warming supper. Always by the roadside at night, a fire burning and a pot of something nourishing to eat. If Granda caught a rabbit in a trap, they ate like kings.

Eventually, Mary and Patrick McDonagh were able to purchase a donkey and cart, and a tarpaulin for a bender tent. Things were much improved with a little less walking, and somewhere to keep their few belongings. The donkey cart was perfect for carrying the big pot that Mary cooked her stews in. The very same pot she was still using.

Rosie always got sleepy listening to Nana's stories and went to bed thinking how much easier her life was compared to how her Nana's had been. Tomorrow, Granda was going to show Rosie how to make a bender tent. Maybe she could sleep out in it. Houses really weren't Rosie's thing. After all, she was a Romany girl. Born to be a traveller.

The Man in the Long Black Coat

The young man hurried from the churchyard, he walked away at such speed that his open, long black coat, flew out behind him like a flag. As he walked through the small town, he could feel the townspeople watching him. Past the busy newsagents, the butcher's shop, with the overpriced meat in the window, all neatly arranged on trays and decorated with garish green, plastic parsley. Then the bakery with its 'buy three, get one free' offer on doughnuts, the sign, plastered across the window. Tempting the weak-willed dieters no doubt. Finally, he came to the empty shop with the To Let sign above the window. He stopped and looked at it for a few moments remembering how, as a young boy, he had gone in to buy sweets.

'Ye Olde Sweet Shop' was always his favourite. He remembered the jars of brightly coloured sweets, all lined up neatly, side by side on the wooden shelves. Pear drops, Sherbet Lemons and Chocolate Caramels with their shiny silver wrappers. Yes, he remembered that shop well.

He carried on walking, away from the town, and towards the moors. He walked away knowing he was still being watched. Jake Wellings began the walk to his home high up on the moors.

Many would consider it an arduous trek, but to Jake, it was just home. The rocky and uneven ground beneath Jakes' feet was smooth as silk to him. He was as sure-footed as a mountain goat. He knew every stone and pebble, every nook and cranny of the windswept moors. This was his domain.

He stopped and sat on a large boulder. From this seat that nature had provided Jake could see the small town. He turned his head away, choosing instead to look at the gorse bushes, the ever-changing brackens and the windswept trees, each one leaning the same way, looking as though a gentle tap could send them tumbling like dominoes.

Jake had sat on this boulder many times. It was 'his' boulder. This is where Jake came whenever he sought solitude. The first time was when he was carried, kicking and screaming into his grandmothers home. He didn't want to be there. He ran off and found 'his' boulder then. His grandmother was a reclusive cave dweller, and he didn't want to live with her. Of course, in time that did change, and he grew to love her very much.

When he found out his parents didn't want him, he sought solace by sitting here watching the hawks circling above him, soaring when they caught a wind thermal. Every time he fell out with his grandmother he would come here and procrastinate. Then he would slope back home knowing nothing more would be said. And today, the day he buried his beloved grandmother. Jake Wellings looked around him. The sky was grey and heavy, hanging low over the moorland. Even the constant chatter of the birds and the screeching of the hawks was missing. It seemed the moors were mourning the loss of the old lady too.

Jake, aged twenty-three years, sat on his boulder and sobbed, he sobbed for the loss of the only woman who had ever truly loved him. Jake's grandmother had lived in the cave on the moors her whole life long, as had her mother before her. She went into the small town occasionally, usually to buy a few necessary provisions and to deliver her herbal remedies to her customers.

Mr Round the butcher was a regular customer. He suited his name. He was a very rotund man and due to his unhealthy eating habits, suffered rather badly with flatulence. Grandmother would make peppermint tea for him to ease his suffering. Telling him to sip the warm brew. Or, she would advise chewing a clove or a few caraway seeds after eating.

Mrs Shewry was another 'patient' of the old lady. She lived in a small cottage on the edge of the moors and had suffered all her life with catarrh. She swore by Grandmothers remedies, and always ensured that she had a regular delivery of powdered Elderflower, Ribwort or Slippery Elm. These powders were steeped in boiling water and made into tea. Occasionally, on the advice from Grandmother, Mrs Shewry would add honey and lemon to the tea, to aid the clearance of her nasal passages.

Jake always went out with his grandmother, to help her find the ingredients needed to make her herbal remedies. From a young age, Jake was taught how to recognise the plants that were needed. Wild Thyme, Comfrey, Borage and Wild Garlic to name but a few. He went out regularly with, and without, his Grandmother, and foraged for the free herbs that grew in profusion on the wild moors. Any herbs required by Grandmother that didn't grow naturally on the moors, she would grow from seed.

Each growing season Jake would be sent out by Grandmother to fetch small buckets of rich peat from the moorland. She would use this to set her seeds. As his Grandmother became infirm with the passing years, Jake took on more and more of the responsibility to produce the herbal remedies. Eventually, Grandmother could only watch as Jake went about his business.

Jake had always been a keen student when it came to learning about herbal remedies from his Grandmother. Not so keen when it entailed going to school. He wanted to be up on the moors, the wind blowing in his face, smelling the earth and listening to the birdsong. He didn't want to be cooped up indoors, that wasn't him at all. So he didn't go. But he couldn't go home either, Grandmother told him school was important. Instead, Jake would hang around the town, dodging in and out of shops, hiding around corners, anything to avoid being seen by the truancy officer that patrolled the town, or worse, someone who might know his Grandmother. Her disapproval he feared more than anyone.

Eventually, of course, Jake was caught by the truancy officer and marched back to school. A letter, care of the Post Office, was sent to his Grandmother informing her of Jake's bunking off. As expected, Grandmother didn't rant and rave at Jake. That wasn't her way. Instead, she sat him down and quietly explained that she hadn't had any education, told him how lucky he was to have an opportunity to learn and that he should grasp that opportunity with both hands. To his credit, Jake listened to the woman who had his best interests at heart. He knew she was right. But why, he wondered, did classrooms have to be so stuffy.

He promised his Grandmother he would continue his schooling and there would be no more bunking off. True to his word, Jake continued going to school. He proved to be a bright student. His interest in his Grandmothers natural remedies fuelled a need to learn more. When he showed a natural aptitude in plant biology, his teacher encouraged him to look into the possibilities of studying at college, to further his knowledge. Jake discussed the prospect of college with his Grandmother, she encouraged him to think seriously about what he wanted to do. Jake wanted to make his Grandmother proud, but could he really suffer college, and more studying?

He was a loner, school friends didn't exist for him. Caveman and Eco Freak were names that followed him through school. His peers didn't understand the ways of the land, had no idea that even some conventional medicines were plant-based. Had they taken the trouble to get to know him then maybe they could have visited the home on the moors that he shared with his Grandmother. The interior of the cave was warm, snug and cosy in winter. In summer, cool and airy. Of course, there was no electricity. No water. Candles and a fire gave them light and heat, the pools of clear water on the moors gave a plentiful water supply. It was a happy home.

The two things, other than his lifestyle, that set Jake apart, was his hair, and his coat... His hair was long and black, and his young skin tanned from life outside. His coat, like his hair, was long and black. He loved the jacket. It was a gift from his Grandmother, and he had cherished it from the moment he had received it.

The townspeople had treated the boy suspiciously ever since he had been living with his Grandmother, after all, what kind of child wasn't wanted by his own parents. There must be something terrible about him. They never considered that the fault could lie with his parents. Two immature youngsters who could barely look after themselves, never mind a child.

Jake's grandmother felt she had let her own son grow wild on the moors, she had let him down. In caring for his son, her grandson, she hoped to make amends. Thinking of his future, Jake made his decision. He discussed it with his Grandmother. It was an easy decision for him to make. He couldn't give this life up. The moors were where he belonged. He was part of them. He would carry on with his Grandmothers work, helping to ease the suffering of others. His Grandmother accepted his decision readily. She knew that he, much like herself, could not leave the moorland. It was in their blood.

Now, today, six years after Jake had made the decision to stay, he had said his final goodbye to his Grandmother. The church had been full. The people of the town had thought very highly of their old herbalist, and they all paid their respects. Time had helped them to accept their young herbalist too. The Man in the Long Black Coat as he was affectionately known, also served the town well.

He had a steady flow of clients, all ready to try his remedies. Some had even visited him and his Grandmother in their moorland home. Curiosity probably playing its part.

Jake had been overwhelmed at how many were in church, even more so at the end of the service, when they all quietly left, allowing him to say a private goodbye. As he left the churchyard, Jake knew that he was watched by people who genuinely felt his loss and that they would understand why he couldn't stop and talk as he would usually have done. Tomorrow he would thank them all. The Man in the Long Black Coat would always reside on the moors, but now, he also had a sense of belonging in the town too. Life was good!

Rosie and Jake's Story

The bell above the door tinkled gently, and Jake smiled to himself. He remembered the sound so well from his childhood. Ye Old Sweet Shop was finally his. Since Jakes grandmother had died seven years ago, the shop had been leased twice. The first time it was a small craft shop that was used well, but the owner grew bored and closed it. The second time it became a pet grooming parlour. That didn't last too long either. Now, after it standing idle for six months, thirty-year-old Jake had taken the shop on, deciding he could now afford it, and, it was time to broaden his horizons.

There was a small flat above the shop, Jake would rent that out, knowing the regular income would help towards the monthly payments that he would be making for the shop. Jake looked around and thought, with a great deal of pride, how pleased his grandmother would be, seeing her remedies packaged so neatly and prettily, and sitting in rows on the new wooden shelves. He had gone to great lengths in choosing the packaging for the natural remedies, wanting them to reflect the moors, where most of the ingredients still came from. With this in mind, he went for muted shades of pink and purple to match the colour of the heather that grew in such abundance, and green and copper to reflect the ferns and shrubs.

This was the final check before opening. Jake had employed a local girl to work in the shop, and he had personally taught her what remedies helped which ailment. Also had a list printed up in case she forgot.

Jake himself was still happiest on his beloved moors. He chose to spend most of his time foraging for ingredients and generally enjoying the feeling of calm that the moors offered him, and of course where he felt closest to his adored Grandmother. He knew she was in the warmth of the sun, the scent of the bracken and heathers and the gentle breeze on summer days. She was never far from Jakes side.

Then there was Rosie. Three years after leaving Ireland, and her maternal grandparents, Rosie and her parents came back to a changing England. They carried on with their travelling ways, but jobs were scarce, and it caused Rosie's parents to think about settling. Friends had settled on permanent sites around the country, where travellers could put down roots and still be amongst the traveller community. Eventually, the decision was made to go to Kent and meet up with fellow travellers who had settled, and hopefully, to see if this way of life would suit Rosie's parents.

Passing through a pretty moorland town, with its picturesque church, Rosie's parents decided to set up camp for a few days on the edge of the moor. It would give Spirit, Rosie's now ageing horse, a rest, and provide the travellers with a chance to stock up on fresh foodstuffs and maybe even sell a few trinkets.

Rosie herself couldn't wait to get high up on the moors amongst the heather and feel the wind in her raven coloured hair. Noticing 19-year-old Rosie's glances towards the moors, her father laughed. 'Rosie, your mother and I can set up camp. Take your sketchbook and pencils and go, I can see you will be no use to us here while the birds call to you from high up there.' Rosie smiled at her father. She didn't need telling twice.

Jake was sat on 'his boulder' procrastinating as usual. Jake was a great thinker these days, and where better to think than out on the moors, his moors. Gazing around him he spotted the girl jumping from rock to rock. She was a distance away, but Jake could see she was sure-footed and used to the rocky surfaces below her feet. Not many climbed the moors with the ease in which she was showing.

He watched until she went from his view. Jake ambled back to his cave home, foraging as he went, a few Borage stems making sure there were flowers on the stems that he could sprinkle into his salad, some sprigs of wild Marjoram and Comfrey.

As Jake neared the cave, he thought he heard a yell. He stopped and listened, but with the wind rustling the leaves on the trees, and the hawks mewling to each other it was difficult to make out individual sounds. However, to Jake, the sound he heard was not a usual sound on the moors.

He stood and listened intently, nothing more could be heard other than the sounds that Jake hears every single day. He carried on home, and on arrival, settled himself down to relax, but he couldn't rest, the noise he heard out on the moors was troubling him, he kept thinking of the girl he'd seen. Maybe it was her. Jake decided to go out and have a wander, just in case. He had only been out for a few moments when he heard the definite shout of 'Hello, can someone help me?'

Jake stood still and shouted back, 'Where are you?' In doing this, Jake hoped for a reply which would help him to work out roughly where the person was.

'I'm over here,' answered a disembodied voice. Jake turned around and began walking in the direction from which the voice came. 'I'm on my way,' shouted Jake. 'Are you hurt?' He was aware that as long as he could ask questions and receive responses, he could follow the sound and find the person quickly.

'I think I'm OK,' came the reply, 'but I'm stuck.' Although Jake was aware that it could be a dangerous situation, he allowed himself a little chuckle. Stuck where, on what, how? He wondered. In no time at all he found himself in front of the young woman he had watched earlier, clambering over the moors with such ease. She was sitting on the ground looking up at him. Jake's heart skipped a beat as he looked into the most beautiful, big, brown eyes, and, as she gazed up at him, he felt as though she was looking into his very soul.

'What happened?' Enquired Jake, as he crouched down rather than tower over her. He was aware that with his long black coat, his long dark hair and his height, he might seem like some mysterious force hovering over her. That was the last impression he wanted to create.

'It was silly really, just put my foot awkwardly on some loose shale and as it moved my foot slipped into the rabbit hole. It refuses to come out,' she stated. 'It seems wedged solid', then added, 'I'm so sorry to be a nuisance.'

'Nonsense.' Responded Jake with a smile, 'We'll soon have you back on two feet.'

Jake started to scrape the soil away from the sides of the rabbit hole making it wider, after a few minutes enough dirt had been removed, and he was able to gently pull her foot free from the hole. Offering his hand, Jake helped her up. As she placed her foot to the ground, Rosie shouted 'OUCH.' In a flash, Jake swept her up in his strong arms and said he would carry her back to his home where he could see the damage to her foot. Rosy tried to explain that it wouldn't be necessary, she could hobble back to her parent's caravan. Jake wouldn't hear of it, and Rosie did feel very safe in this man's arms.

She relaxed as Jake began the short walk back to the cave. 'Oh, wait, my sketchbook.' Said Rosie, 'I left it by the rabbit hole, I can't leave it behind.'

'Don't worry Miss erm?' Jake laughed, and Rosie noticed, not for the first time, how Jake's eyes sparkled. 'I'm Jake Wellings, and you are?'

Rosie smiled, 'I'm Rosie Perkins, pleased to meet you Jake Wellings.'

'Likewise Rosie Perkins.' Jake told Rosie his home was here on the moors, reasonably close by. Once he got her comfortable he would run back and fetch her sketchbook, it wasn't too far away and would come to no harm.

Rosie wondered where Jake's home was, she couldn't recall seeing any buildings that may have resembled a home as she'd wandered the moors. As she was thinking so he announced, 'Here we are Rosie, home sweet home.' They were at the entrance to Jakes cave. 'Oh, this is different,' exclaimed Rosie. Entirely unfazed by Jakes unusual home. They entered the cave, leaving the warmth of the sun behind them. Once inside the living area, Jake settled Rosie on the large sofa. 'May I look at your foot, Rosie?' Asked Jake. Rosie lifted her leg up off the sofa as, once again, she protested to Jake that she could sort it herself. 'If I have sprained my foot or ankle, Hyssop and Marjoram will help it, if it's just bruising,' explained Rosie.

'You can use Arnica oil' stated Jake, finishing off Rosie's sentence. Rosie looked surprised. 'Oh, you know about herbs and how they heal!'

'Yes,' smiled Jake. 'I know about herbs, and the sooner we get something for your foot, the sooner it will begin to feel better.'

'My sketchbook? Asked Rosie.

'Will be fine,' responded Jake, as he gently massaged Arnica oil into her foot.

After removing her shoe, and flexing her foot, Jake noticed there was no swelling and minimal discomfort to Rosie with her foot movement. He concluded that the foot was indeed, just bruised and the Arnica oil would help. Jake made Rosie a camomile tea, then informed her he was going to recover her sketchbook from by the rabbit hole, where it had been left. He told her he would not be long.

While Jake was gone, Rosie gazed around her, taking in the wonderful surroundings that was Jakes home. A cave home. She loved it. True to his word, Jake soon collected the abandoned sketchbook and a small case holding Rosie's coloured pencils.

He wondered what she sketched, but refrained from looking inside. Maybe she would show him if he asked. It was the first thing Jake did ask as he returned it to her. 'What do you sketch Rosie? It's a talent I envy in anyone who can draw anything more than a stick man.'

Rosie laughed and handed Jake her pad. 'Here, see for yourself,' she said, still laughing. Jake sat for quite a time browsing Rosie's artwork, saying nothing. Finally. 'WOW! WOW! WOW! These are wonderful Rosie, what a talent you have.'

Jake had twenty questions for Rosie. 'The gypsy caravan is perfect in detail, your flowers look as though they could be picked from the page. Who are the people? Are those buildings in your hometown? Where did you study? Which Art college did you go to?'

'So many questions,' stated Rosie. 'But I have to go, my parents must already be wondering where I am.'

Jake stood up. 'Of course, you are on holiday, will your foot be alright to walk on? I will walk with you to the town, we don't want you finding another rabbit hole.' In truth, Jake just wanted to spend more time with Rosie. He was enamoured with her natural beauty, her talented drawing skills and the natural, relaxed manner in how she spoke with him. He felt he had known her forever.

'My foot will be fine Jake, thank you, and I will be sure to avoid the rabbit holes.' She smiled warmly at him, 'and thank you for looking after me. My parents will probably want to thank you too.'

Rosie was reluctant to leave, she was enjoying the company of the cave-dwelling man. 'Perhaps you should walk me down the moors, just in case.' Said Rosie. 'Then I can answer your questions on the way.' She smiled, and her whole face lit up. Jake was smitten. This girl wasn't like any other he had met before. She didn't seem to mind that he lived in a cave, that he didn't have all 'mod cons' and a traditional dwelling. He believed he would live his life alone because, like his Grandmother before him, he could not, and would not, leave the moors. The women Jake met were fascinated by his chosen way of life, and impressed at his knowledge of his surroundings, but, was the way of life a way for them? The answer was always the same. No! Could he dare hope that Rosie was different?

As the pair slowly walked back down the moors towards the town, Rosie told Jake about her sketches. The people were her parents and her late Grandmother. Jake noticed her sadness when she spoke of her Grandmother, how her eyes misted over. He laid his hand gently on her arm and said quietly, 'I understand your sadness Rosie, I lost my own Grandmother, I lived with her here, on the moors, she was my teacher, and my friend as well as being my Grandmother. After all this time I still miss her.' Tears fell down Rosie's cheeks as she said, 'Oh Jake, I am so sorry, I didn't mean to stir up old memories and make you sad.' Jake cupped her face with his hands and brushed her tears away with his thumbs. 'You didn't make me sad Rosie, I don't believe you could.' She smiled through her tears at him, and they continued their slow walk off the moors.

Jake spotted the colourful caravan at the edge of the moorland first. 'We don't see many of those around here, what a beauty, very similar to the one in your sketchbook Rosie.'

'It's the very one Jake, this is home.' Stated Rosie. 'I'm a Romany girl. I have been a traveller my whole life.'

'So that's how you know about the herbs and their benefits,' laughed Jake. You have grown up with them, the same as I did.' As the pair reached the caravan, Rosie's mother came out. 'There you are Rosie, we were starting to worry, you were gone a long time.'

'Sorry, I didn't mean to worry you, I got my foot caught in a rabbit hole and couldn't get it out.' Rosie said.

Looking at Jake, Rosie smiled and said. 'Mum, this is Jake, he freed me from the rabbit hole. I would probably still be there if he hadn't.

'Are you ok, did you hurt yourself?' Rosie's mother fussed around her.

'I must thank you Mr?' Jake held his hand out to Rosie's mum. 'Jake Wellings pleased to meet you, Mrs Perkins.' '

Where's Dad?' Rosie asked, wanting Jake to meet him too. 'He won't be long, replied Mrs Perkins, he met someone in the town earlier, looks like he may have some work for a while. We could be staying a bit longer than the planned few days. Jake could hardly contain his pleasure. 'That's great, I could show you around the town Rosie, and more of the moors, if you wanted of course. There are plenty of things to sketch.'

'Oh I would like that Jake, thank you.' Rosie wondered if she sounded a little too eager. 'Come on Jake, come and meet Spirit, my horse, then my dad should be back, and you can meet him too.' Rosie grabbed Jakes hand and pulled him along. 'He's just over here.' Her sore foot, seemingly forgotten. Rosie's mum watched her daughter, and, smiling to herself, she thought she had never seen her so happy and relaxed with anyone who wasn't well known to her.

At nearly twenty years old Rosie's mum had been married two years, and Rosie herself was six months old. Rosie and Jake found Spirit grazing quite happily, untethered, by the roadside. Spirit knew he was loved and well looked after. Nothing would induce him to run off, and a life spent on the road meant traffic didn't spook him. Rosie told Jake all about the Appleby Horse Fair, how her dad bought Spirit for her when she was only eight years old. She told of how she gathered heather for her Grandmother, who would then bind the stems with white ribbon, selling the lucky heather wherever they went. Jakes interest encouraged Rosie to tell him more of her life as a traveller, and the more he heard, the more enamoured with Rosie he became.

Eventually, Rosie's dad arrived back with the news that the work he had been offered would last possibly two weeks. This was music to Jake's ears, he hoped it meant he could spend more time getting to know Rosie. Rosie wasn't disappointed either. After being introduced to Rosie's dad, Jake asked him the nature of the work he had secured for himself. Mr Perkins told him it was a woodcutting job in a wood store. The owner, Charley Samms, had a big order that he needed to get out and he was two men down. One man was off sick, and another was on holiday.

Jake told Rosie's dad that Charley was a good boss and a man well thought of in the town. He would be treated fairly. Jake was invited to stay for supper, an offer he declined, but finally accepted at the insistence of Rosie and her parents. A thank you for rescuing Rosie from the rabbit hole.

The lamb stew that Rosie's mother produced was like nectar on Jakes taste buds. It had been a long time since he had tasted such well-cooked food. Not since the last meal his Grandmother had cooked for him. She had taught him to cook, but it was never the same. Jake wondered to himself if Rosie cooked as well as her Mum. As if she were reading his mind, Rosie's Mum smiled at Jake and said, 'Yes, she does.'

The two weeks went by very quickly, and, true to his word, Jake had shown Rosie around his town. He had shown her the pretty church and its churchyard where his Grandmother rested. Rosie had popped back later and placed a bunch of wildflowers on her grave, feeling confident the old lady would appreciate it. Jake had told her so much about his Grandmother that Rosie felt she knew her. She met some of the townspeople, Jake's customers, she had sketched the church and other buildings. Together they had walked the moors or just sat amongst the heather enjoying the sheer beauty of the nature that surrounded them. But all good things end eventually, and they both knew that the two blissful weeks were over and they must say goodbye in the morning, maybe never to meet again.

It was now or never thought Jake, as they sat side by side in the moonlight. 'Rosie, please don't go, stay here with me. I know I have fallen in love with you, and I can't bear for us to be apart. I will look after you and keep you safe. You will have the freedom of the moors, just say you could be happy here.'

Jake was aware that he was talking at a million miles an hour, but if he stopped, he couldn't say what he had to say. Rosie sat quietly for a moment, then got up and walked away from Jake, towards the camp-fire where her parents were. Jake put his head in his hands, he'd said too much, he thought. She obviously didn't feel the same, and he had frightened her off. He felt annoyed with himself and very embarrassed. He stood up just as Rosie's dad came up to him. 'Mr Perkins,' Jake said. Jake wanted to explain himself, but Mr Perkins raised his hand and said, 'Jake, you and Rosie have our blessing, we could see from day one that you two were meant for each other. Just couldn't work out why you both took so long to realise it yourselves.'

Jake took a last look around the shop and then stepped out into the street, locking the door behind him. He looked down the street as his two favourite girls walked towards him. Rosie, his wife, and Flora, their two-year-old daughter.

Flora was named after Jake's Grandmother and was a beauty like her mother. Hand in hand the three of them walked towards home. Life was as good as it could be thought Jake. He thought that he was quite definitely the luckiest man alive.

Printed in Poland
by Amazon Fulfillment
Poland Sp. z o.o., Wrocław